Praise for the Novels of Phillip Margolin

"The best one yet!"

—*Red Carpet Crash* on *The Darkest Place*

"Readers are in for a great ride . . . with one surprising what-the-hell-is-going-on-here moment after another. . . . This is not only the best in the series but one of Margolin's best novels, period."

—*Booklist* (starred review) on *The Darkest Place*

"In the hands of Phillip Margolin, nothing is ever simple and no one is really safe. He is the master of the suspense mystery."

—Associated Press on *Executive Priviledge*

"This may sound silly to say about a writer of Margolin's consistency and productivity, but . . . this may be his best novel ever."

—*Sullivan County Democrat* (Callicoon, NY) on *The Darkest Place*

"Margolin is a wizard who creates a story that brings all the issues to a neatly trimmed head. If you have nothing to do for two days, pick up *The Darkest Place*—you won't be disappointed."

—*New York Journal of Books*

"Legal-thriller fans will find it satisfying to see Margolin back at the top of his game . . . his writing has regained its stylistic flourishes, and his pacing is impeccable."

—*Booklist* on *The Perfect Alibi*

"Packed with surprises all the way to the end."

—*Fresh Fiction* on *The Perfect Alibi*

"This is one book you will not be able to put down."

—*Bookreporter* on *The Third Victim*

"Thoroughly engrossing." —*Criminal Element*

"What makes his books interesting is the ability to intertwine facts about the justice system within a riveting plot."

—*Military Press* on *The Third Victim*

"Margolin knows how to pack in the thrills!"

—Tess Gerritsen on *Sleeping Beauty*

"Exceptional!" —*Booklist*

"It takes a really crafty storyteller to put people on the edge of their seats and keep them there. Phillip Margolin does just that." —*Chicago Tribune*

"Skillful plotting, good writing, and an excellent cast of characters." —Nelson DeMille on *Wild Justice*

ALSO BY PHILLIP MARGOLIN

Heartstone
The Last Innocent Man
Gone, But Not Forgotten
After Dark
The Burning Man
The Undertaker's Widow
The Associate
Sleeping Beauty
Lost Lake
Worthy Brown's Daughter
Woman with a Gun
Vanishing Acts (with Ami Margolin Rome)

AMANDA JAFFE NOVELS

Wild Justice
Ties That Bind
Proof Positive
Fugitive
Violent Crimes

DANA CUTLER NOVELS

Executive Privilege
Supreme Justice
Capitol Murder
Sleight of Hand

ROBIN LOCKWOOD NOVELS

The Third Victim
The Perfect Alibi
A Reasonable Doubt
A Matter of Life and Death

THE DARKEST PLACE

Phillip Margolin

St. Martin's Paperbacks

Published in the United States by St. Martin's Paperbacks, an imprint of St. Martin's Publishing Group

THE DARKEST PLACE

For information, address St. Martin's Publishing Group, 120 Broadway, New York, NY 10271.

www.stmartins.com

Library of Congress Catalog Card Number: 2021044038

ISBN: 978-1-250-84983-0

Our books may be purchased in bulk for promotional, educational, or business use. Please contact your local bookseller or the Macmillan Corporate and Premium Sales Department at 1-800-221-7945, ext. 5442, or by email at MacmillanSpecialMarkets@macmillan.com.

Printed in the United States of America

Minotaur hardcover edition published 2022
St. Martin's Paperbacks edition / November 2022

10 9 8 7 6 5 4 3 2 1

DEDICATION

Writing a book is exciting and thoroughly enjoyable, but it is also a lonely business. I spend every day in my office with the blinds drawn and the door shut, staring at a computer monitor. That's why I love book tours. I get to mingle with readers and answer their questions, and independent bookstores are my favorite places to do a signing.

Ever since Covid struck, independent bookstores have been fighting for their lives. Forbidden to let readers in to browse the shelves, they have had to invent ways to survive. I live in Oregon, and I am happy to report that my favorite stores are still in business and starting to reopen.

The Darkest Place *is dedicated to all of the nation's*

independents who gutted it out. Thank you on behalf of readers everywhere for fighting so hard and staying alive against the odds.

PART ONE

MURDER WITH BENEFITS

JANUARY–FEBRUARY

CHAPTER ONE

Portland homicide detective Roger Dillon drove down the gravel road past run-down shacks and the occasional double-wide as a soggy January rain spattered the windshield of the unmarked car. His partner, Carrie Anders, scanned the roadside mailboxes and front doors for the house number they were seeking.

Carrie was a large woman who was as strong as some of her male counterparts. She spoke with a slow drawl, leading people who didn't know her well to form the impression that she wasn't too bright. That gave the college math major an edge.

Roger Dillon was the opposite of Carrie in every way except IQ. A slender African American with close-cropped salt-and-pepper hair, Dillon was almost twenty years Carrie's senior and several inches shorter. He had been one of Portland's most successful homicide detectives since his promotion over twenty years ago.

The road curved, the houses disappeared, and the detectives found themselves penned in by towering evergreens on a narrow stretch of smooth, freshly paved asphalt. Three minutes later, they rounded another curve.

"What the hell is that?" Dillon asked.

"I'd say that we've just discovered the winner of the world's ugliest house contest," his partner replied.

Standing on a wide, manicured lawn was a three-story McMansion that was as out of place in rural, economically depressed Profit, Oregon (population: 2,467), as a Rolls-Royce Silver Cloud in an Afghan slum.

The driveway circled a grotesque fountain that was an obvious copy of one from a famous Las Vegas casino. Roger parked, and the detectives ran through the rain to the shelter provided by a portico, where they faced an oversized front door decorated with stained glass. Strewn across the multicolored panes by an inept artisan were stags that looked like dogs with horns and trees that could have been the creation of a first-grader.

Carrie rang the doorbell. The chimes played the opening notes of the theme from *Jaws.* The detectives started to laugh. Then they remembered why they were here.

A shadow moved toward them behind the stained glass. Moments later, a tall woman with a trim, athletic build, pale blue eyes, and long blond hair secured in a ponytail stared at the odd couple. She was wearing jeans and a dark blue cable-knit sweater.

"Are you Mrs. Joel Loman?" Carrie asked.

"Marjorie Loman, yes."

The detectives displayed their credentials, and Carrie introduced them. The woman frowned.

"How can I help you?" she asked.

"Can we come in?" Carrie asked.

The woman hesitated. Then she stepped aside, and the detectives entered a massive entryway lorded over by an immense, crystal chandelier.

"Is there somewhere we can talk?" Carrie asked.

The woman led Roger and Carrie into a cavernous living room past a white grand piano to a sofa draped with colorful Mexican blankets. A pair of high-backed armchairs upholstered in burgundy leather sat in front of an enormous fireplace. Mrs. Loman took one of the armchairs and gestured toward the sofa.

"What's this about?" she asked when the detectives were seated.

"I'm afraid I have some very bad news for you, Mrs. Loman," Carrie said. "Your husband has passed away."

Marjorie stared at Carrie for a moment as she processed this information. "Do you mean he's dead?" she asked.

Carrie nodded.

Loman covered her mouth for a moment. Then she broke out laughing. "That's the best news I've had in months." The detectives looked at each other. "Did the bastard overdose on cocaine, or did his girlfriend stab him?"

"He was shot," Carrie said. "A homeless man found the body in back of a Portland restaurant. There are signs that he was tortured."

"Huh," Marjorie said without any emotion. "Have you arrested the guy who did it?"

"We're just starting the investigation," Carrie answered.

"You don't seem very broken up," Roger said.

"You wouldn't be either if you were married to Joel. We were getting divorced, and it hasn't been pretty. He looted our accounts and hid the money. I had to change the locks to keep the bastard from sneaking in while I was at work and stealing the furniture. If he had his way, I'd be homeless like the guy who found him, which might not be a bad alternative to living in this monstrosity."

"You don't like your house?" Carrie asked.

"You're joking, right? I hate it. We both grew up in Profit, and Joel had to show the whole town how big he'd made it. Now that he's dead, I'm going to sell this eyesore, if anyone is stupid enough to buy it."

"How did Joel make his money?" Carrie asked.

"Good question. I know he worked the stock market and was some kind of investment counselor, but he was always evasive when I asked him for specifics."

"Did he have enemies?"

"I'd be shocked if he didn't, but I don't know anything about his business and very little about his so-called friends."

"Why did you marry him, if you dislike him so much?" Carrie asked.

Marjorie sobered. She looked down at the Persian carpet and into the past. "We were high school sweethearts, and we married young. We were both pretty wild, and the crazy stuff we did then seemed like fun. Now, not so much."

When she looked up, Marjorie looked sad. "Everything was okay until Joel started making money and hanging with what passes for the jet set in Portland. That's when I became old news."

She shrugged. "I guess he didn't think I was fun anymore because I didn't want to snort cocaine or do threesomes or drink all night until I passed out."

"Can you think of anyone who can help our investigation?"

"Kelly Starrett is his partner, in more ways than one."

"Pardon?" Carrie said.

"Joel and Starrett ran Emerald Wealth Management, and he was banging her, so she can tell you more about his business and his social life than I can."

"Are you going to be okay by yourself?" Carrie asked. "Do you want us to call someone, a friend, family?"

Marjorie shook her head. "I've got work in an hour. That will keep me busy."

"What do you do?" Roger asked.

"I do what you do. I'm a cop on the Profit police force."

The detectives talked to Marjorie Loman for another half hour. When their car was out of sight, Marjorie took out her phone.

"McShane and Freemont," a receptionist said.

"This is Marjorie Loman. I need to talk to Greg McShane."

"Hey, Marjorie," a man said moments later.

"Two detectives were just here. Someone killed Joel. They found his body behind a Portland restaurant."

"Jesus!"

"Yeah. They said he was tortured."

"That's horrible. Do they have a suspect?"

"They said they don't. So, look, now that Joel's dead, can he still hide our money? Because I'm almost tapped out."

"You're still Joel's wife, so it's all yours, if we can find where he hid it."

"Can you do that, find the money?"

"I'll call Kent," McShane said, mentioning Joel's attorney. "I'll see if he knows where Joel hid the assets. Now that Joel is dead, he'll have no reason to keep it secret."

Marjorie called the Profit Police Department and told her sergeant about Joel. He told her to take as much time off as she needed to deal with the funeral and her grief.

As soon as she disconnected, Marjorie went to their well-stocked liquor cabinet and poured herself a glass of Joel's very expensive single-malt scotch. She was just topping off the glass when McShane called.

"I have good news and bad news."

"Give me the good news."

"Joel converted most of your assets to gold bars and stashed them somewhere. The good news is that you can claim the gold because you're still Joel's spouse."

"Did Kent tell you the name of the bank?"

"That's the bad news. Joel wouldn't tell him where he hid the gold."

"Is it in Oregon? Because we can hire someone to ask around."

"Kent says the gold could be anywhere in the world."

"You're shitting me."

"I wish I were. Has Joel taken any trips lately?"

"I have no idea. He's been living in Portland since we separated, and I've only seen him when it was absolutely necessary. Can you help me find out where that asshole stashed my money?"

"I can put some people on it, but you should go to Joel's place in Portland and see if you can find some clue to where he hid the gold."

CHAPTER TWO

Robin Lockwood had spent the last week on a beach in Hawaii with Jeff Hodges, her investigator, celebrating their engagement. Instead of working on a motion that was due by the end of the day, she was admiring her diamond ring when her receptionist told her that Harold Wright was on line two. Robin's mood morphed from happy and content to wary.

"Hello, Judge," Robin Lockwood said. "To what do I owe the honor of this call?"

"I need a favor," the Honorable Harold Wright said.

Judge Wright was one of Robin's favorite judges. He was fair, very intelligent, and had a great courtroom demeanor, but he used Robin as a go-to when he had a case that no one wanted to accept on a court-appointed basis.

"I'm listening."

"I need an attorney to represent Lloyd Arness. You may have heard about the case."

"The rape?"

"Yes."

"There are many attorneys on the court-appointment list. What's so special about me?"

"I won't beat around the bush. Every attorney I've called has turned me down. I need someone with guts to take the case, because you will be cursed and reviled by the press and every decent citizen if you represent Arness."

"Gee, Judge, thanks for handing me this fabulous opportunity."

"I usually don't lecture attorneys about civics, but I have always believed that it's the worst criminals who have to get the best trials. If citizens see that a horrible serial killer, who everyone would personally execute, is treated fairly by our justice system, then they will have faith in the system if they're arrested for shoplifting or drunk driving. When people lose faith in the system, we get the French Revolution."

Robin laughed. "Jesus, Judge, talk about overkill. Please stop before I shoot myself."

"I guess that was a bit much."

Robin was quiet for a minute, and the judge let her think.

"Okay," she said finally, "but you have to promise to fix my parking tickets."

Now it was Judge Wright's turn to laugh. "Not a chance. But I will promise not to make fun of some of your more outrageous motions before I deny them."

That was the last lighthearted moment in Robin's representation of Lloyd Arness.

Robin was five foot eight with a wiry build. Her eyes were bright blue, and she had a straight nose, high cheekbones, and short blond hair that framed an unmarked oval face. That was significant because she had earned part of her tuition at Yale Law School by fighting in mixed martial arts bouts on televised pay-per-view events in Las Vegas. During her representation of Lloyd Arness, Robin had to use every ounce of self-restraint to keep from beating her client to a pulp.

The police had to piece together what had happened in the Harkness home on the evening Marianne Harkness was attacked because she had been left with permanent brain damage. The puzzle had started to come together after fingerprints and DNA led to Arness's arrest, and it spelled out proof beyond a reasonable doubt when Lloyd supplied the missing pieces by bragging about the rape in great detail to the acquaintances who had ratted him out and the detectives who interrogated him.

The detectives had done everything right, and Robin decided that there was no way she could keep Lloyd's statements to the police from a jury. Absent an act of God—which she did not see any decent God delivering to a despicable cretin like Arness—Robin could not imagine winning the case at trial. That, Robin decided, was what she was going to tell Arness when they met at the jail. Hopefully, he would fire her and ask for new counsel.

A guard let Robin into one of the contact visiting rooms at the Multnomah County jail. The room was solid concrete with a large pane of bulletproof glass through which a guard could watch for dangerous behavior. Robin took a seat on a plastic chair on one side of a metal table that was bolted to the floor. Moments later, a guard led Arness in through a thick metal door at the back of the room.

Lloyd Arness was a slim, well-muscled man with a shaved head and evil tattoos. As soon as the guard left, he settled onto the chair on the other side of the table and grinned at Robin.

"I see they gave me the sweetest-lookin' lawyer in the bar. When I'm acquitted, you and I should spend some time together."

"I'm afraid that an acquittal is not going to happen, Mr. Arness. I've read the police reports, and the State's case is as tight as I've ever seen. You left your fingerprints all over the bedroom, you were foolish enough to rape Mrs. Harkness without a condom, so there's DNA galore, and the police have your graphic confession."

"In which I clearly say that the bitch consented to screw me, so there wasn't no rape. Hell, she told me I was the best she ever had."

Robin stared at her new client. "At the end of most consensual sexual encounters, the female doesn't need plastic surgery and isn't left with permanent brain damage."

"That weren't me. She was purring like a kitten when I left her. Maybe she didn't watch where she was going and fell down the stairs. Or—and this is what I think happened—she told hubby how she'd been royally fucked, and he beat her up."

Robin pushed a stack of papers across the table. "This is the discovery I received from the DA. It sets out the State's case. Read it. The next time I visit, I'll have the State's plea offer, and we can discuss the pros and cons of taking it."

Arness looked amused. "So, that's it. All I get is ten minutes of your precious time?"

"If you have questions, I'll be glad to answer them."

Arness looked Robin up and down. "I would like to know the color of your panties."

Robin refused to rise to the bait. "I believe in being honest with my clients. I took your case because no other lawyer in town wanted to come within a mile of you. After reading the police reports, I can see why. But I have represented terrible people before, and I have always given my best efforts. That is what you'll get from me. What I want from you is a promise to keep a civil tongue in your head."

Robin rang for the guard. As soon as she was out of the contact room, she felt like dousing herself in disinfectant.

When Robin arrived at Barrister, Berman, and Lockwood, she went to Jeff Hodges's office. Jeff was six foot two with shaggy reddish-blond hair, green eyes, and pale, freckled skin that still bore faint traces of scars from an explosion in a meth lab he had raided when he was a Washington County police officer.

"Fucking Harold Wright!" Robin swore the moment she was seated across from her fiancé.

Jeff was shocked. Robin had grown up in Elk Grove, a very conservative farming community in the Midwest, and she rarely cursed.

"What did His Honor do now?" Jeff asked.

"He begged me to take a court-appointed case, and I accepted, and I'm now saddled with having to defend the slimiest, most disgusting cretin in Oregon."

"Considering the slimeballs you've represented, that's saying something," Jeff said as he fought to suppress a smile. "What's Mr. Cretin alleged to have done?"

"You can drop the 'alleged' part," Robin said. And she proceeded to tell Jeff about the rape of Marianne Harkness, and the joy Lloyd Arness took in it. When she finished, Jeff wasn't smiling.

"What are you going to do?" Jeff asked.

Robin sighed. "What I always do—give our client the best defense."

"I assume you'll try to get a plea deal from the DA, because this sounds like one of the surest bets for a conviction in history if it goes to trial."

Robin nodded. "I just came here to vent. I'll be on the phone to the DA as soon as I go to my office. The problem is Arness. He denies the rape, and he's such a narcissist that I'll bet he'll demand a trial, so he can wow the jury with his personal charm."

"I'm guessing that you don't think he has a 'wow' factor."

"Lloyd Arness is the most repulsive . . . thing I have ever met."

CHAPTER THREE

Before Joel broke the news to Marjorie that they were through, he'd purchased a penthouse in Northwest Portland. Marjorie knew that her lawyer would tell her not to go at night because Kelly Starrett would probably be there, but she wanted to see the skank's face when she learned Joel was dead.

Moments after Marjorie rang the bell, the door was opened by Starrett, a six-foot blonde who ran marathons, practiced yoga, and drained Joel's bodily fluids. She looked like a slightly younger, more toned version of Marjorie, who was amazed that Joel had swapped her for a woman who looked so much like her.

"What are you doing here?" Starrett asked.

Marjorie pushed past Starrett and walked into the

living room where Adele's voice was enhanced by state-of-the-art speakers.

"Where do you think Joel is?" Marjorie asked.

"Manhattan."

"Buzz. Wrong answer. He's in the county morgue."

"What are you talking about?"

"Some good Samaritan killed him and dumped him in an alley, so no divorce, which means that I am now the proud owner of all of Joel's worldly goods, including his fuck pad. Do you have any clothing, toiletries, or other possessions stowed here? If you do, I'll give you twenty minutes to clear out."

"Listen, you . . . ," Starrett said as she took a threatening step toward Marjorie, who took out her service revolver and pointed it at Starrett's chest.

"I'd think twice before attempting to assault an officer of the law in her newly acquired property."

Starrett stopped dead.

"Good thinking. Now, before you get your shit and get out, I have a question for you. Joel emptied our bank accounts and converted the money to gold. Do you know where he stashed it?"

"If I did, I wouldn't tell you."

"That's what I figured. But you should think about who you're talking to. I had a very pleasant talk with my lawyer, and he assures me that I am now part owner of your firm. He'll be in court first thing in the morning to tie up every one of your assets."

The color drained from Starrett's face, and Marjorie smiled. Then she looked at her watch.

"You now have nineteen minutes and twenty seconds to clear out. Anything that's left, I burn, starting with the sheets."

Starrett hesitated. Then she walked toward the bedroom slowly, her shoulders thrown back, in an attempt to maintain her dignity.

"Oh, yeah, one more question."

Starrett froze.

"Don't worry, I'll pause the timer. Did you kill Joel? If the answer is yes, you can stay here and be my new best friend."

Marjorie recognized murderous rage when she saw it, and she was glad Joel's partner didn't have a weapon. Starrett glared at Marjorie for a second before storming into the bedroom.

Marjorie smelled an odor wafting toward her from the kitchen where Starrett had been cooking a vegan stir-fry. She turned off the stove, dumped the stir-fry down the disposal, and waited for Starrett to leave. Eighteen minutes later, the front door slammed. As soon as she was alone in the apartment, Marjorie searched every inch, looking for clues to where Joel had hidden their money. When she was through, she called Greg McShane.

"I just went through Joel's penthouse, and I didn't

find anything that shows where he hid the gold. What do I do now?"

"I'll have to think about that. I may have to hire an investigator to track it down."

"I'm really hurting for cash, Greg. Outside of my salary, I have nothing. How long will that take?"

"I have no idea."

"Great," she said sarcastically.

"I'm sorry I can't give you a timeline. Kent thinks Joel was very careful about covering his tracks."

"Yeah, okay, thanks. I know you'll do your best."

CHAPTER FOUR

Elk Grove was just recovering from a storm that had been pummeling the Midwest. The blanket of snow sparkled in the sunlight and made the town square with its ice-frosted gazebo and frolicking children look like a Christmas card.

On the surface, Elk Grove seemed to be doing okay. The Anderson Meatpacking plant was a national brand and provided steady employment for a good portion of the community, the high school was always competitive in sports and sent its share of graduating seniors to prestigious colleges, and local businesses did not have to compete with a big-box store. But, if you looked hard enough, you could see that all was not well in Elk Grove. Family farms were barely making it, and there were many vacant storefronts on Main Street.

Caleb and Emily Lindstrom were employed by the meatpacking plant, where Emily was an accountant and Caleb worked as a foreman. Emily had a boyish figure and short, dirty-blond hair. She was plain looking, but her smile, which had captivated Caleb, could light up a room.

Caleb towered over his spouse the way he'd towered over opposing players when he'd anchored the Elk Grove High offensive line. But he was a gentle giant, quick to laugh and equally quick to lend a hand.

The Lindstroms drove to work together every morning, and they returned home together every night. They had met at the plant, their five-year marriage was a happy one, and they had only one regret.

Caleb took his lunch break at noon in the cafeteria with Archie Duncan, who'd played next to Caleb on the line and had been best man at his wedding.

"You should have seen Adam and Aaron on Saturday," Archie crowed. "They both had ten points, and Aaron was a demon on defense."

Archie was always bragging about his twins, who starred on the fourth-grade basketball team and brought home excellent report cards. He never noticed that Caleb had to force a smile when he was going on and on about the boys.

"Kids are such a blessing, Caleb. When are you and Emily gonna get around to starting a family?"

This was a question that Caleb dreaded. It wasn't as if he and Emily hadn't tried, but they had been unsuccessful. Last week, the couple had learned why.

"We'd like to," Caleb confided to his best friend, "but we just found out it's not gonna happen."

Archie could read the pain on Caleb's face, and his smile disappeared.

"What's the problem?"

"We've been trying, you know, and everything is great in that department," he assured Archie as his face turned red with embarrassment. "But we went to a specialist when Emily didn't get pregnant, and, well, she can't do it. There's some kind of problem."

"Hey, Caleb," Archie said as he laid a hand on his friend's shoulder.

"We see how much fun you and the rest of our friends have with your kids, and, well, it hurts."

Suddenly, Archie looked thoughtful. "I just had an idea. You know Rick Santoro?"

"Yeah?"

"He and his wife had the same problem, and I heard that Darrell Holloway helped them get a baby."

"Isn't Holloway the lawyer who advertises on billboards and bus benches?"

"Yeah."

"He does DUIIs and divorces."

"That's the guy."

"How did Holloway help Santoro get a baby?"

"I have no idea."

"We talked it over, and Emily and I don't want to adopt."

"No, it was something else. You should give him a call."

CHAPTER FIVE

Two days after Joel Loman's murder, Roger Dillon and Carrie Anders took the elevator up to Emerald Wealth Management, which occupied the top floor of a twenty-story building in downtown Portland. The waiting room was done up in polished wood, gleaming chrome, and floor-to-ceiling windows that gave its customers an unimpeded view of the sky. Roger guessed that Emerald wanted its investors to imagine their greenbacks soaring upward and out of sight.

Roger also imagined that the elegantly dressed receptionist usually greeted visitors with a happy face, but she struggled to look upbeat when he told her that he and Carrie Anders were homicide detectives who wanted to talk to Kelly Starrett.

Moments after the receptionist relayed the message, a well-dressed young man came into the waiting room, told the detectives that he was Miss Starrett's assistant, and led them into an open room where equally well-dressed men and women looked up from their computer screens and eyed the detectives warily. No one looked happy.

Carrie's first impression of Joel Loman's partner was that she was a very attractive woman whose skillfully applied makeup had almost, but not completely, covered up the evidence of a rough night.

"We know this must be a very trying time for you, Miss Starrett," Carrie said, "and we appreciate your taking the time to talk to us."

Starrett stared at Carrie with bloodshot eyes. "Do you know who killed Joel? Because I want to give him a medal."

Starrett pointed through the glass wall that gave her a view of her employees.

"A team of accountants are in a room down the hall trying to figure out how much money my thieving partner has embezzled. When they finish assessing the damage, many, if not all, of these people will probably be unemployed."

"You think Mr. Loman was stealing from the firm?" Dillon said.

"I know that for a fact. What I don't know is how much he stole." She put her head in her hands. "This is a nightmare."

"Can you suggest anyone who might have had a motive to murder Mr. Loman?" Carrie asked.

"Do you mean besides me?"

Carrie smiled. "Yes."

Starrett sighed. "His wife is the obvious suspect. They were in the middle of a brutal divorce, and she hated Joel."

"Did Mr. Loman tell you this?"

"When she came to the apartment I shared with Joel and kicked me out at gunpoint, she made her feelings about Joel crystal clear."

"What about clients? You must have some who've lost money and blamed you or Mr. Loman."

"Of course, but I can't think of anyone who struck me as homicidal."

The detectives talked to Starrett for twenty minutes more. Then Carrie handed Starrett her card.

"Thanks again for talking to us. If you think of anything that might help us find Mr. Loman's killer, please call."

Starrett took the card. Then she frowned. "There is one thing. Joel leased a Mercedes. He had a reserved parking spot in the garage right next to mine, but the car isn't there."

CHAPTER SIX

Darrell Holloway's office was a storefront in a strip mall. An elderly secretary invited the couple to sit on a stained and cracked, pea-green Naugahyde couch while she announced their presence. Fifteen minutes later, Holloway came out of his office with a smile on his face.

"Sorry to have kept you waiting, but I was wrapping up a big settlement in a PI case. Terrible auto accident." The lawyer shook his head sadly. "Horrible injuries. But you don't get the big bucks unless there's a real tragedy." Holloway stopped abruptly and shook his head. "But you don't want to hear about my cases, and I do want to hear about your problem. Come on into my office."

Holloway's joy at profiting from a client's horrible

injuries had upset Emily, and the lawyer's appearance was not reassuring. He was unnaturally thin with a sallow complexion, what remained of his hair was swept across his skull in an inadequate comb-over, and a wisp of a mustache covered his upper lip.

The lawyer's clothing matched his physical features. His sports jacket showed signs of wear and tear, his slacks didn't go with the jacket, and his white shirt had a coffee stain on the collar. To put it mildly, Holloway did not inspire confidence. Neither did his office, which looked like it had been furnished at garage sales.

Holloway motioned the couple onto client seats and dropped onto a high-backed chair that stood behind a scarred wooden desk.

"So, how can I help you two?" Holloway asked as he flashed an ingratiating smile.

Caleb looked uncomfortable. When he spoke, his words came out in a rush.

"Emily and me want to have kids. In vitro didn't work, and neither has anything else. Then, last week, we took some tests. They came back bad, and our doctor said it wasn't gonna happen for us. So, I have a friend who heard that you helped the Santoros get a baby, and we wanted to find out how you did that."

Holloway nodded. "Okay. Well, I'm sorry about your situation, and you understand I can't discuss what I've done for other clients. But I do have a suggestion."

"Go ahead," Caleb said.

"Have you heard about surrogacy?"

Caleb frowned, but Emily nodded. "You pay a woman to have your baby?" she said.

"That's right," the lawyer answered. "You use the husband's sperm to impregnate the surrogate mother, so part of your baby has the father's genes, and you get the baby right away, the day it's born. So, the baby has love and affection from the get-go."

"I have a question," Emily said.

Holloway smiled. "Ask away, and don't be shy. I know this is a big and scary step, and I'm here to make sure you have all the information you need to make a sound decision."

"I think I've read about surrogates who change their mind at the last second or sue for custody or visitation. There would be nine months of building up our hopes. It would kill us to have it all come crashing down."

"That would be awful, and that's why we have the surrogate sign away her parental rights at the start. There's a contract, and it guarantees that the surrogate can't change her mind after taking your money. In fact, we make sure that the surrogate never even gets to hold the baby after the delivery, so she can't bond with it."

"Just how much money are we talking about?" Emily asked.

"I'm not going to sugarcoat this. It's going to be expensive. You pay the surrogate ten thousand dollars when she signs the contract and forty thousand dollars when the baby is delivered. Then there's a monthly allowance plus health insurance, life insurance, and a promise to pay medical bills."

Caleb looked sick.

Holloway nodded. "It's a big investment."

"What kind of woman does this?" Emily asked.

"I always get that question, and I can guarantee you that we are not talking about prostitutes or people with addiction problems. The women we choose are clean, smart, and respectable. I'm talking about students who need the money to pay for college, single women with financial problems. You don't have to worry. We screen the surrogate very thoroughly for mental and medical problems, so you can be certain that you'll be getting a healthy baby."

"You've given us a lot to think about," Emily said.

"Of course. I never expected you to decide right now. Go home and think about what you want to do. I'm always here to answer your questions, and I'll do whatever it takes to help you."

"Do you trust Holloway?" Emily asked when they were in their car on the way home.

"He seemed . . ."

"Shady?"

"Yeah. I don't know if we can trust him, but he did sound like he knew what he was talking about."

Emily was quiet for a while. Then she said, “Fifty thousand dollars is a lot of money.”

“He said the surrogate wouldn’t get most of it until after we had the baby. And he did get the Santoros a baby.”

“According to Archie.”

“I can call Rick.”

“You should do that.”

“We could take out a second mortgage on the house,” Caleb said. “My folks might help out. You know how much they want grandkids.”

Emily looked sad. “The baby wouldn’t be mine, Caleb. It wouldn’t have any part of me.”

“Aw, honey, that’s not true. It wouldn’t have your genes, but it would have your love, and you would have so much say in what kind of person he becomes. Look at how many natural mothers mess up their kids. Biology is part of a child, but love is more important.”

Emily went quiet, and Caleb let her think, because he needed to get his head around the idea of hiring a surrogate mother too.

“I’ve done the math,” Emily said when they were parked in their garage. “We’ve been smart with our finances, and we’re making good salaries. We wouldn’t have to get the full fifty thousand from a second mortgage, and we can definitely handle the monthly allowance and the insurance requirements.”

Caleb turned to face Emily. "Does that mean you want to hire a surrogate?"

"It means we can handle the money part. I still want to think about the rest of it."

Caleb placed a hand on his wife's shoulder. "I love you more than anything, Em. All I want is for you to be happy. And this is too important a decision to just jump into. Let's think it over. I'll call Rick, and I'll do whatever you decide."

CHAPTER SEVEN

Marjorie didn't want to sit around at home the day after she took possession of the penthouse, so she worked her normal shift. It was dark when she arrived back at her McMansion. She headed for the living room and was about to settle down with a drink when the door-bell rang. Marjorie put down her glass and walked to the front door.

Two men were standing on her welcome mat. They were dressed in suits, but they didn't look comfortable in them. What they did look was intimidating. Both men were huge. Their shoulders stretched the seams of their jackets. One man's head was bald and twice as big as normal. One eyelid drooped, and the lobe of his left ear was missing. The other man was smaller, with a full head of auburn hair, but still oversized and just as scary.

"Can I help you?" Marjorie asked.

"Are you Joel's wife?" the bald man asked with a soft, incongruous lisp that made him sound like Mike Tyson.

"Yes."

"May we come in?"

"Not until you tell me what you want."

The big man smiled, revealing a gap in the top row of teeth. "We want the money your husband owes us."

Marjorie barked out a humorless laugh. "Join the club. Joel and I were in the middle of a divorce, and he sucked all the money out of our accounts and hid it. So, we're both out of luck."

"Now that Joel is dead, you'll have to make good on his debts, including this one," the redhead said.

"If Joel owed you money, why should I be responsible?"

"That's not the question you should be asking. You should be asking how you can get us our money, so you don't end up like Joel."

"Threatening me isn't going to help. I just told you that Joel hid our money, and I have no more idea where it is than you do."

"Then you'd better get an idea real fast or face the consequences."

Marjorie's features hardened. "If you know Joel, then you know I'm a cop. So, I'd go easy on the threats."

The bald man laughed. "You're a cop in Profit, Oregon. That ain't exactly LA. Last I heard, you didn't have a SWAT team."

"And no one is threatening you," the redhead said. "We're simply suggesting that you clear up your ex-hubby's financial affairs, because it's in your best interest to do so."

"How much money are we talking about?"

"We are talking about a quarter of a million dollars, Mrs. Loman," the redhead said.

"Who are you?" Marjorie asked, forcing herself to sound calm.

"We're people you don't want to fuck with," answered the bald man.

"We'll give you a week to get our money," the redhead said. "The next time we ask for it, we won't be so polite."

The men left. Marjorie locked the front door. Her hand shook as she downed her drink. Then she refilled the glass to the brim and dropped onto the nearest chair.

What had Joel gotten involved in? Then it dawned on her that it really didn't matter. It was going to take a long time before she would see any of the gold, and the men who had just threatened her didn't seem like they had a lot of patience. Marjorie dialed Greg McShane.

"Hey, Marjorie. What's up?"

"I've been thinking about ways to solve my money problems. Selling the penthouse and my house would get me some quick cash. Can you handle that?"

"That might not be possible. Kent phoned a while ago with some disturbing news. There's a problem at Emerald."

"What kind of problem?"

"Joel may have been stealing from the company."

"What does that have to do with me?"

"If there's litigation and he's stolen his clients' money, assets like the penthouse and your house could be tied up."

"Shit! This just gets better and better."

"I just found out about Emerald. I'll need more time before I can advise you on what to do."

"Yeah, I get that. Thanks, Greg. I apologize if I was short with you."

"No need. I know how tough this is for you, and I'll do my best to help."

Marjorie downed her drink. While she refilled her glass, she ran through several scenarios. There was no way she was going to get her gold anytime soon, and selling the penthouse and her home might not be doable, which meant those men would be visiting again. After giving her situation some thought, Marjorie Loman decided that there was only one thing she could do.

CHAPTER EIGHT

Vanessa Cole was a trim African American in her midfifties with sharp features, brown eyes, and a law degree from Stanford. After joining the Multnomah County district attorney's office, Vanessa had worked her way to a top position in the criminal division because of her brilliant performances in the courtroom and her high ethical standards. When her boss had to retire because of health problems, the governor had followed his advice and appointed Vanessa to be the Multnomah County district attorney. In November, she had been elected to the office.

"What's up?" Vanessa asked with a welcoming smile when Carrie Anders and Roger Dillon walked into her office.

"There's strangeness in the town of Profit, Oregon,

and we need your help to figure out what's going on," Roger said.

"Profit isn't in our county," Vanessa said.

"True, but the dead body of Joel Loman, its richest citizen, was found behind a restaurant in Portland a few days ago," Carrie explained.

"Do you have any suspects?"

"Two as of now, but there may be a lot of people who wished Mr. Loman ill. He ran a boutique investment firm with Kelly Starrett, who doubled as his mistress. She said that she checked the books as soon as she learned Loman was dead. It seems that the late Mr. Loman was an embezzler."

"How much did he steal?" Vanessa asked.

"Starrett isn't certain, but it could be millions."

"Who is your other suspect?"

"Marjorie Loman, his widow. We interviewed her soon after the body was discovered. She couldn't have been happier when we told her that her husband had been tortured and killed."

"They were in the middle of a divorce, and it wasn't amicable," Roger interjected.

"We had some more questions for Mrs. Loman, so we went back to her house," Carrie continued. "No one was home. I walked around the place, but all the doors were locked. We peeked through the mail slot, and there was mail building up in the entryway.

"Mrs. Loman works for the Profit Police Department. I talked to her sergeant. He said she was on leave because of her husband's death, and he hadn't seen her since her last shift.

"Kelly Starrett said Mr. Loman drove a Mercedes he leased for the business, and she said it was missing. Mrs. Loman drives a Volvo, and it wasn't at the house. We put out an APB for both cars. The Mercedes turned up in a parking lot at the Portland airport. We haven't found the Volvo yet. We impounded the Mercedes, and we need a warrant to search the car and Loman's house."

Carrie handed Vanessa an affidavit in support of a search warrant. Vanessa looked up after she read the affidavit.

"Consider it done," she said.

CHAPTER NINE

The line Darrell Holloway had fed the Lindstroms about settling a big PI case had been pure BS. Business had been slow, and Holloway was just scraping by. When the Lindstroms called and said they wanted him to find them a surrogate, it was the first piece of good news he'd had that month.

The Lindstroms were going to bring the fifty thousand in tomorrow, and he'd told them that he would hold it in his trust account. He hadn't told them about the contract he had with the surrogate in which he received ten thousand dollars for arranging the match, and he was definitely not telling anyone that he was going to dip into his portion as needed, even though it would be illegal to take the Lindstroms' money out of the trust account without their permission. Once baby Lindstrom was born, no one would care.

There was nothing on Holloway's desk that needed his immediate attention, so Darrell decided to walk down the block and celebrate his good fortune at the Elk Grove Tavern.

Holloway let his eyes adjust to the darkened interior. Then he walked to his favorite stool at the end of the bar. Max Rheingold, the owner and bartender, started to put a beer in front of the lawyer, but Holloway held up a hand.

"Make it a Johnnie Walker Black Label, Max. I'm celebrating."

"Settled a case, did you, Darrell?" Rheingold asked.

"New client."

Max moved toward the bottles of scotch. When Holloway turned his head to watch him, he noticed the woman sitting two stools from him. She was attractive and well-dressed, and she was nursing a drink while she focused on the top of the bar. Holloway hadn't gotten laid in a while, and he was feeling lucky.

"Hi," he said. "I haven't seen you here before. Are you new in town?"

The woman turned her head slowly. "Did you get that one out of *Pickup Lines for Dummies*?"

Holloway was feeling too good to be offended, so he laughed. "It wasn't intended as a pickup line. Elk Grove is pretty small, and I was just being friendly."

The woman looked embarrassed. "Sorry. I'm just having a bad day. Yeah, I just got into town last week."

"Can I buy you a welcome drink?"

The woman hesitated. Then she said, "Sure, if there are no strings attached."

Holloway moved to the stool next to the woman and asked her what she was drinking. Then he gave the order to Max.

"I'm Darrell Holloway. I'm an attorney. My office is just down the block."

"Ruth Larson."

"Where'd you move from?"

"Florida," the woman answered without elaborating.

Holloway studied Larson. He guessed that she was in her thirties. She had short brown hair, pale blue eyes, smooth skin, nice teeth, and manicured nails, but she didn't have a Florida tan.

"Are you here visiting relatives?"

"No."

"Elk Grove isn't exactly a tourist destination. And the weather is sure different from where you're from. So, what brings you to the cold and snowy Midwest?"

"A bad divorce."

"Divorce is one of my specialties, and I know they can be rough."

"Too true."

"You said you were having a bad day. Anything I can help with?"

"Not unless you want to hire me."

"What type of job are you looking for?"

"Anything. I've spent the past week putting in applications at the meatpacking plant and a few other places. No bites so far."

Ruth didn't strike Holloway as the type of woman who would want to work in a meatpacking plant, and that gave him an idea.

"I'm not surprised you're having a hard time finding work. Times are tough in Elk Grove, and jobs are difficult to come by, but I might be able to help. I do know about a job that pays well, but it's a bit unusual."

PART TWO

THE DARKEST PLACE

OCTOBER–NOVEMBER

CHAPTER TEN

Robin Lockwood and Jeff Hodges were in a great mood when they walked through a light rain toward the Multnomah County Courthouse for Lloyd Arness's sentencing, because Lloyd Arness would no longer be a client after today.

The hearing was being held on an afternoon in early October, and the previous eight months had been spent giving her all for a trial Robin knew she would lose, losing that trial when the jury returned a verdict of guilty in record time, and feeling only relief that Lloyd Arness would be locked in a cage for a long, long time.

Robin's long legs drove her through the rain at a fast pace. A limp was another remnant of the meth lab explosion, and Jeff had to work hard to keep up with his fiancée.

After completing a one-year clerkship on the Oregon Supreme Court, Robin had been hired by Regina Barrister, a brilliant criminal defense attorney. When Regina retired because of the onset of dementia, she had made Mark Berman and Robin, her two associates, partners in the firm.

Shortly after joining Regina's firm, Robin found that she was attracted to Jeff and he was attracted to her. Wary of an office romance, neither one did anything to encourage intimacy, but they couldn't deny the mutual attraction, and eventually they had become lovers. Several months ago, Jeff had suffered a serious injury while they were investigating a murder case. Robin realized how deeply she loved him, and she had proposed marriage in Jeff's hospital room. He had accepted gladly, and they were planning their wedding.

"Once I get this sentencing out of the way, I won't have anything pressing until the Getty trial starts in December," Robin said. "I'm up to speed on Getty, so I think it would be a great time to go to Elk Grove for a week, so you can meet my family."

"That is a terrifying suggestion," Jeff joked.

"They won't bite, and Mom is dying to meet you."

"What if she doesn't approve?"

"You'll charm her. And I need time to work out the details of the wedding with her. Every time we talk on the phone, the plans get more and more grandiose. If

I don't bring her back to earth, the wedding will cost millions."

"What will I do while you two are fighting over the menu and the seating arrangements?"

"You'll spend quality time with my brothers and their families, during which they will reveal all the awful things I did as a teenager."

"You told me your brothers are all champion wrestlers. What if they decide I'm not good enough for you—which I'm not—and they decide to beat me up?"

"Don't worry, dear. I'll protect you."

Jeff smiled. Then the courthouse came into view, and he sobered. "Look, Robin, I want you alert as soon as we go inside. Kevin Harkness has been threatening to kill our client, and you need to take the threats seriously."

"I do, and so does Judge Wright and Vanessa. They've told me that there's going to be extra security."

"I can't blame Harkness for wanting to kill Arness," Jeff said. "He's an animal."

Robin was in complete agreement with Jeff. She'd regretted her decision ever since she'd accepted the court appointment. Her client had no regrets about the rape and enjoyed reliving it. He'd also treated his trial as if it were a reality television show.

Judge Wright held court on the fifth floor of the Multnomah County Courthouse. Robin and Jeff took the elevator to five and were mobbed by reporters as soon as they entered the corridor outside the courtroom. Robin repeated, "No comment," mechanically as she and Jeff fought their way inside. Several reporters followed and found seats in the packed spectator section. Jeff sat behind Robin on the aisle.

Moments after Robin was seated at the counsel table, two guards escorted Lloyd Arness out of the holding area, and the spectator section began to hum with muted conversations. Robin's client was manacled because he'd tried to escape during a pretrial hearing, but he didn't seem to mind. The convicted rapist surveyed the courtroom with a big grin like a rock star looking over his audience. Then he focused on Robin.

"How you doin', beautiful?" he asked before running his tongue over his lips and leering.

Robin looked at Arness with disdain until the rapist broke eye contact and laughed.

"Can't get a rise out of you, can I, Counselor? Course that might change if I ever got you alone."

Robin was tempted to make an ego-deflating response before remembering that she was a professional in a courtroom and not a two-year-old on a playground.

"Grow up, Lloyd," Robin said.

Arness laughed again just as Judge Wright took his seat on the dais, and the conversations in the spectator section ceased. Robin stood next to her client.

Judge Wright started to say something when someone screamed.

Robin turned toward the spectator section. A man was pointing at one of the sheriff's deputies. Someone else yelled, "He's got a gun!" Robin was confused. *Why wouldn't a deputy have a gun?* Then it dawned on her that the gun was pointed at Arness, and the man pointing it was Kevin Harkness.

Harkness fired. Spectators were screaming and running for the door. The shot hit Arness in the head. Robin raised her arm across her face to deflect the spray of skull fragments and brain tissue, so she didn't see the weapon shift toward her.

Before Harkness could pull the trigger, Jeff smashed into him, knocking him to the floor. As Harkness and Jeff wrestled in the narrow row between the seats, Robin heard two more shots mixed in with the sounds of the fleeing crowd. The court guards separated Jeff and Harkness, wrestled the gun from the distraught husband, and handcuffed him.

Then the guards looked at Jeff. His hand was over his stomach, and he was taking deep, rasping breaths. Blood was seeping through his shirt and spreading between his fingers.

Robin raced to Jeff. It took several guards to restrain her. She screamed as she fought against the arms that held her. Then she collapsed and began to sob when she realized that the love of her life might die.

* * *

When Robin arrived home, she could barely function. She had spent hours at the hospital on the edge of panic as surgeons fought to save the most important person in her life. Then she had wandered home in a fog after a doctor found her in the waiting room and told her that his team had lost its battle. Jeff was dead.

Robin opened the front door and walked into their apartment. Only it wasn't *their* apartment anymore. Jeff had made this space a happy place that was a haven from the stress of Robin's job. Now he had gone away forever.

Robin collapsed on the couch. It seemed impossible that they would never make love again or lie in bed laughing and cuddling or sit together on this couch holding hands while they watched TV.

The dam broke. Tears streamed down Robin's cheeks, and her chest heaved with each heartbreaking breath. Jeff was dead, Jeff was dead. The thought ricocheted through her mind, but she could not grab hold of it. Jeff couldn't be dead. They were going to get married. How could he be dead?

After a while, Robin stopped crying. She shut her eyes and leaned her head against the back of the couch. It would have been wonderful if she'd fallen asleep and escaped from reality for even a short time, but sleep would not come even though she was exhausted.

Robin had no idea of how much time had passed

when she took out her phone. It was several hours later in Elk Grove, and it took a while for Shirley Lockwood to pick up.

"He's dead, Mom," Robin sobbed over and over.

CHAPTER ELEVEN

The events at the funeral barely registered. Robin felt as if she were in a theater watching a movie. Jeff's parents had passed away, but his sister, her husband, and their children attended. Robin accepted their condolences mechanically, forgetting them as soon as they were uttered.

Robin felt numb as she listened to the eulogies. When the service was over, Robin's brothers and their wives surrounded Robin. Her mother, Shirley Lockwood, took her arm and started leading Robin out of the church. Vanessa Cole stopped Robin halfway up the aisle.

"I understand you're going home for a while," the district attorney said.

Robin nodded.

"Take all the time you need. I talked with Mark. He and your associates will work on your cases while you're gone. I know there will be some cases that require your personal attention. I'll set those over until you come back."

"Thank you," Robin managed, although she had lost all interest in her cases.

Vanessa gave Robin's shoulder a gentle squeeze and stepped aside to let her move on.

It took a while to get to the car that would take Robin to the cemetery because her friends, judges, attorneys, and court personnel stopped Robin every few feet to give her their heartfelt condolences. Robin knew they meant well, but she just wanted the day to end, so she could take a sleeping pill and fade away.

Robin had not cried in church, and she didn't cry at the cemetery when they lowered Jeff into his final resting place. It felt like there was a Plexiglas shield between her emotions and what was going on around her.

A light rain had fallen at the cemetery, and Robin thought that God must be shedding tears for Jeff. Then the graveside ceremony ended, and her mother ushered her to a waiting car.

Robin stared out of the window during the ride to her apartment, but nothing really registered. When her mother tried to interest Robin in dinner, she begged off.

"I'll pack for you," Robin's mother said as she tucked her daughter into bed.

"Thanks, Mom," Robin said, slurring her words as the sedative kicked in.

"We'll fly home in the morning," Shirley said, but Robin's eyes were already closed.

The flight to the airport in the capital was a blur, as was the hour-and-a-half ride from the capital to Elk Grove. Robin's hometown had not changed much since she'd left for college. There was a dusting of snow on the town square, but the sidewalks on Main Street were clear. The marquee in front of the high school advertised a basketball game against Mill City. Jack, her oldest brother, said a major winter storm was expected. Robin didn't care and continued to stare out the window. Jack started to say something else about the weather, but stopped when he realized that Robin needed to be in a quiet place.

The Lockwood farmhouse was painted blue with yellow trim and kept in good repair by her mother and brothers. A front porch looked out over a lawn that would stay brown until the spring. Robin climbed the steps and waited for her mother to open the front door. Then she walked to the second floor without a word. Jack followed with her luggage, and her mother followed Jack.

"Do you want something to eat?" Shirley asked.

"Not right now. I'm kind of tired."

"Okay. You take a nap. I'll fix something when you're ready."

The door closed, and Robin sat on her bed. Little had changed in her room since high school. The trophy she'd won for placing third in the boys' district wrestling tournament in her senior year at Elk Grove High decorated the top of the dresser, and framed newspaper articles about her third-place finish and her lone win at States that year hung on the walls.

In Portland, everything she saw reminded her of Jeff. Robin had hoped that getting away from the city would help, but it didn't. It just made her more depressed. Here in her old room, she felt like every day of her life since she'd graduated from high school had been erased.

CHAPTER TWELVE

Ever since she'd agreed to be the Lindstroms' surrogate, Marjorie Loman had been living in a cheap garden apartment, pretending to be a woman named Ruth Larson. Elk Grove was one of the dullest places in the universe, and she'd been bored out of her skull, but now that her contractions had begun, she could see an end of her sentence in purgatory. Unfortunately, Mother Nature was placing an obstacle in her path.

The local television anchors were calling it "the Storm of the Century," and it was living up to the hype. Outside her apartment, the drifts were starting to assume the shape and size of a mountain range, and there was no sign that the snow would let up. Marjorie had no interest in the weather because the pain from her contractions was all-consuming.

Marjorie had called Darrell Holloway when her water broke, but he didn't answer his phone. She thought about calling the Lindstroms, but the pain was so intense and the contractions so frequent that she knew she had to get to the hospital.

During the previous nine months, Marjorie had gotten friendly with her next-door neighbor, a divorced woman in her fifties, who had given birth to three children. As soon as Marjorie explained that she was in labor, the woman helped her into her pickup and took off for the hospital. Even with chains and all-wheel drive, they barely made it through the blinding snowfall on the ice-slicked roads.

The neighbor had called ahead, and an orderly was waiting with a wheelchair when they parked in front of the emergency room. A nurse accompanied Marjorie as they sped down the corridor to the delivery room.

The pain was excruciating, and Marjorie prayed that the thing inside her would leave, but she could not evict it. Marjorie did not think of the growth in her uterus as a person. It had been a source of money for nine months and nothing more; an *It,* to which she had no emotional connection and whose expulsion would result in a payday.

Finally, after an eternity in labor, the doctor extracted the baby with forceps. Marjorie sobbed with relief, thinking that would be her final contact with

It. Nancy Cleary, the nurse who had assisted with the delivery, was jet-lagged after flying back from a vacation the day before and exhausted from fighting the storm to get to work, and she missed the note in the chart that explained that "Ruth Larson" was a surrogate who was not supposed to have any contact with the baby once it was delivered.

When Marjorie was taken to the recovery room, the nurse followed with the baby. When the nurse laid the child on Marjorie's breast, she was too weak to protest. Then the tiny lips closed on her nipple and began to feed. After a while, she found that she enjoyed comforting the baby, and a smile formed on her lips.

The next morning, the hospital got through to Darrell Holloway. Holloway phoned the Lindstroms to let them know that their bundle of joy had arrived. The snow had stopped falling, and the snowplows had cleared the main roads. Holloway was waiting for his clients when they rushed into the hospital waiting area, looking happy and nervous.

"Congratulations!" Holloway said, grinning as if he were the proud father. "You are the parents of a perfectly healthy baby boy."

"When can we see him?" Emily asked anxiously.

"There's a waiting room down the hall. I'll go with a nurse, and we'll bring the baby to you."

Holloway parked the happy couple and walked to the room where he'd been told Nancy Cleary was waiting with the baby. Holloway found the room, took two steps into it, and stopped. Marjorie was sound asleep, as was the baby in the bassinet that stood beside the surrogate's bed.

"What is that fucking baby doing with this woman?" Holloway demanded.

Cleary's jaw tightened, and her fingers curled into fists. "I will not be spoken to in that way."

Holloway turned on her. "Your instructions were very clear. This woman is a surrogate mother with zero rights to this child. She was never supposed to be within a mile of the baby once she gave birth."

Cleary paled. "It was an emergency, the storm," she stuttered. "I didn't know."

Holloway forced himself to calm down. "Sorry I got angry, but letting a surrogate bond with a newborn can lead to all sorts of difficulties, including lawsuits against the hospital."

The nurse looked sick.

"Look, let's get the kid away from Miss Larson. The Lindstroms are here to get their baby, and neither of us wants a scene."

Cleary picked up the baby slowly and gently, so he would not wake up, and Holloway followed her down the hall to the room where the Lindstroms were waiting. He was grateful that Larson had stayed asleep, and a scene had been avoided.

"Here's your little darling," Holloway said.

Cleary stepped up to Emily with the baby in her arms. He stirred, and his eyes opened. Emily looked down at her baby, and the baby stared back at her.

"Can I?" she asked the nurse.

Cleary smiled. "Of course."

There were tears in Emily's eyes as she took the baby in her arms. Caleb peered over Emily's shoulder at the ruddy-faced child, who snuggled against his wife's breast.

"We're calling him Roy, after my dad," Caleb said.

Emily noticed that there was a slight swelling on Roy's head.

"Is he . . . Does Roy have any problems?" Emily asked.

"Not a one," the nurse replied. "Your Roy is perfectly healthy."

Emily wiped away a tear and turned toward Holloway.

"Thank you, Darrell. You've made our dreams come true."

Holloway looked down, pretending to be embarrassed. "You know, a lot of a lawyer's work revolves around tragedy—people injured, people facing jail—but it's moments like this that balance out all the hard things we have to do. So, let me thank you for brightening my day."

A tear formed in Nurse Cleary's eye, and Caleb and Emily smiled at their lawyer. Holloway smiled back. He was very, very happy, but his happiness had nothing to do with the Lindstroms or their baby. As soon as he returned to his office, he would be transferring money out of his trust account and into his checking account.

Marjorie Loman woke up slowly. She was still groggy after the exhausting delivery, so she closed her eyes and drifted off. In that happy space between reality and her dreams, she remembered her baby, whom she had decided to call Peter. Peter was so soft and warm, and it had felt so good to hold him.

There had been many reasons for hating Joel, and his refusal to have children had been one of them. They had never talked about children during the first insane years of their marriage, but the partying and the drugs and the drinking had almost destroyed Marjorie.

One horrible morning, after coming down from a cocaine binge, sicker than she'd ever been, she realized that she would die if she didn't get off the merry-go-round. She had tried to get Joel to see where they were headed. He didn't want to hear what she was saying, so they'd taken different paths. She'd sobered up, joined the police department, and started thinking about having a child. Joel had turned his risk-centered, gambler's personality into a moneymaking career in finance and had made it crystal clear that he had no interest in having a house with a white picket fence, two children, and a dog named Spot.

Marjorie smiled. Joel was out of her life for good, and she had a baby. She remembered how wonderful it had felt when Peter's tiny lips sucked on her nipple and the satisfaction she'd felt knowing that her milk was filling him up and keeping him alive.

Marjorie had a plan, and it started with shedding her Ruth Larson identity as soon as she was out of the hospital and paid in full. The baby was a complication, but not one that would derail the plan.

Marjorie turned her head. The bassinet was empty. A nurse must have taken Peter away while she slept. She rang the call button.

"Can you bring my baby to me?" Marjorie asked when the nurse came into her room. Nancy Cleary didn't answer. She looked stricken.

"What's wrong?" Marjorie asked.

"I'll get the doctor," the nurse stammered. Then she left the room.

While Marjorie waited, she imagined the worst. Had Peter died? Was there something wrong with him?

The door opened, and a young woman in a white jacket walked into the room with Nancy Cleary trailing behind. The doctor smiled.

"Hi, Ruth. I'm Dr. West. How are you feeling?"

Marjorie returned the smile. "Pretty good. Where's Peter?"

The doctor's brow furrowed. "Who's Peter?"

Marjorie's smile widened. "I named my baby Peter."

The doctor stopped smiling. She looked uncomfortable. "The baby is with his parents, Ruth. They left with him an hour ago."

"What are you talking about?"

"Didn't Mr. Holloway explain everything to you?"

Marjorie sat up. "Where is my baby?"

The doctor hoped that the situation would not become difficult. "You signed away your parental rights when you agreed to be a surrogate for the Lindstroms. Mr. Holloway assured us that you understood that they would be taking the baby."

"I changed my mind. I want Peter. Get him back!"

"That's not possible."

Marjorie started to get out of bed. Dr. West placed a gentle hand on Marjorie's shoulder.

"Please, Ruth. Calm down."

Marjorie glared at the doctor. Then she slapped her hand away. "Get off me, and get me my baby."

"The child is not . . ." Dr. West started. Marjorie

punched her in the chest. She was weak, and the punch was ineffective. The doctor grabbed her hand, and Nancy Cleary rushed to assist her.

"Please be calm," the doctor begged as they forced Marjorie back onto the bed. Marjorie screamed.

CHAPTER THIRTEEN

"Darrell, we have a problem," Dr. West said when the lawyer answered her call.

"What kind of problem?"

"Ruth Larson is insisting that she wants the Lindstrom baby. I tried to explain that she'd given up her parental rights. She went berserk, and I had to sedate her."

"Shit."

"Exactly. Can you come to the hospital and reason with her? She won't listen to me."

"Yeah, Diane. I'll be right over."

Holloway hung up. He'd forced himself to sound calm, but he was furious that there were complications caused by the idiot that had let Larson bond with the baby. If Ruth Larson caused trouble, it could lead to lawsuits and the possible loss of his fee.

"Hi," Holloway said when he walked into his client's hospital room. "How are you doing?"

Marjorie stared at the lawyer for a moment before tearing up.

"I'm not good, Darrell," she sobbed. "They stole my baby."

Holloway brought a chair over to the side of Marjorie's bed and waited until the surrogate calmed down.

"We talked about this. Right at the beginning, we went over the fact that you were giving up all rights to the baby. You signed papers giving up all parental rights. Do you remember that?"

"Those people . . . They kidnapped Peter. The hospital, all of you . . ."

Holloway felt very uncomfortable. He liked clients who didn't challenge him and paid his fees, and he hated dealing with crazy clients.

"No one is kidnapping the baby." He held out a copy of the paper she'd signed in which she agreed to relinquish her parental rights. "Read this. It's got your signature on it. It's been notarized."

Marjorie grabbed the document, glared at Holloway, and threw it on the floor. "I don't care what some paper says. Peter is my baby."

"No, he's not. He's the Lindstroms' baby, and you'd better accept that."

"I will get my baby back."

"Okay, now listen up. The hospital made a big mistake. You were never supposed to get the baby after you gave birth. And I understand how it felt, having the baby with you. But you've got to accept the fact that you have no legal right to the child, and you can't go near him."

Marjorie decided that Holloway was part of the conspiracy to steal her baby. It was the lawyer, the Lindstroms, the hospital, all of them working together to keep her baby from her. So, she decided that Holloway would just lie if she continued their conversation.

"I'm tired. I want you to go away, so I can get better and get out of this place."

"That's the way to think. You get some rest and stop thinking about that baby, okay?"

"When do I get the money, Darrell?"

Holloway flashed a phony smile. "Come see me when you're rested." He stood up. "I have a client coming over in a few minutes. I just wanted to make sure you were okay and that you were straight about the Lindstroms' legal rights to the baby."

Marjorie didn't say anything, and Holloway made his escape. Marjorie stared at the doorway for a few moments after Holloway disappeared. She hated him, she hated the hospital, but most of all, she hated Caleb and Emily Lindstrom.

CHAPTER FOURTEEN

The storm started to fade away while Caleb and Emily were at the hospital, and it had stopped snowing by the time they drove home. The next day brought temperatures in the high forties, and the snow began to melt. Caleb made a comment about the weather while he fixed breakfast, but it didn't register with Emily, whose undivided attention was on the new addition to the Lindstrom household.

Roy was keeping them up for a good part of the night, but neither parent minded the crying, and they took great joy in being able to comfort their baby. They took turns holding Roy, and they held hands after he fell asleep and they were back in bed.

* * *

Roy turned out to be a calm baby, crying only when he was hungry or needed his diaper changed. Although the Lindstroms had read that the smile of a young infant might be caused by gas, they chose to believe that Roy smiled because he was happy.

Emily had been granted maternity leave, and she was perfectly content to wait on Roy all day. Caleb spelled her when he came home and enjoyed his time with their newborn. The Lindstroms were sleep deprived but as happy as they'd ever been, and the first inkling that their happiness might end came at three o'clock on Saturday afternoon, two weeks after Roy was born.

"Someone's at the door!" Emily yelled from the nursery.

"I'll get it," Caleb said.

When he opened the door, he was surprised to find Ruth Larson on their front porch. Holloway had assured the Lindstroms that there would be no further contact with their surrogate once their baby was born.

"Hi, Ruth, how are you?"

Marjorie didn't correct his use of her alias. "I'm okay," she said.

"That's good. I'm glad. So, what can I do for you?"

"Um, Mr. Lindstrom, I've been thinking about the baby."

"That's kind of you. He's doing fine."

"Yes, well, what I wanted to say is that I want my baby back."

Caleb's heart rate accelerated. "Do you remember that Mr. Holloway explained that you would have no right whatsoever to Roy? This was when we met you for the first time. You signed legally binding papers giving away your parental rights. We all have copies."

"Peter is my baby," Marjorie insisted. "He was in me for nine months."

"Look, I can see this is hard for you, but you're young. You can have a baby of your own. You know how much we wanted Roy. Emily can't have a baby of her own. You know that."

Marjorie's features hardened. "I don't care about Emily. I care about my baby. I want him back."

"Okay, Ruth. I'm going to insist that you leave and that you have no further contact with us. You knew what you were getting into when you signed your contract and took our money."

"You can't buy a baby. It's not legal. I'll go to court and make you give him to me."

"And I will get a restraining order from the police if you don't stay away from us."

Marjorie's hands curled into fists. "You bastards don't deserve my baby. People like you think they can buy anything. My baby isn't for sale."

Caleb started to say something, but realized that it would be useless to try to reason with the woman.

"This conversation is over," Caleb said, and he slammed the door shut.

Marjorie pounded on the door and rang the bell. Emily walked into the entryway. She looked alarmed.

"What's going on?"

"It's Ruth Larson. She wants Roy."

"What?"

"I told her she can't have him."

Marjorie continued screaming through the door, and the bell continued to ring. Roy started crying.

Emily headed for the door. "I'm going to talk to her."

Caleb grabbed her arm. "Don't. She's too angry. Ignore her. Go to Roy, and I'll call Holloway."

Emily hesitated for a moment. Then she left Caleb to comfort Roy. By the time Darrell Holloway answered the phone, the shouts and pounding had stopped. Caleb walked to the front window and saw Marjorie walking away.

"We have a big problem," Caleb said, and he proceeded to tell their lawyer about the surrogate's visit.

"Is she still there?" Holloway asked.

"No. But I'm afraid she'll come back when I'm at work, or she'll sue and drag us into court."

"You don't have to worry about a lawsuit. The contract everyone signed will protect your parental rights. And I'll go over to her apartment and try to calm her down."

"I'll get a restraining order if she comes here again. I'm not going to allow her to upset Emily."

"No, no, you're one hundred percent right. Let me see what I can do. I'll call you and let you know how it went after I talk to Ruth."

Marjorie wasn't in her apartment, so Holloway went to the Elk Grove Tavern and found her downing scotch at the bar.

"We have to talk," he told her.

"Did the Lindstroms go crying to you?"

"Let's go to a booth where we have some privacy."

Marjorie hesitated. Then she got off her stool and carried her drink to a booth in the back of the tavern.

"What did you think you were doing?" Holloway demanded.

Marjorie didn't answer.

"They can have you arrested for trespass or harassment. Do you want to go to jail?"

Marjorie stared into her drink.

"We went over this several times, Ruth. You know that Roy is legally the Lindstroms' baby."

Marjorie looked at Holloway. "I know I haven't been paid. That's breach of contract."

"And I told you that you'd be paid in full very soon," Holloway said as his gut tightened. "I invested some of your money, so you'd have more than the forty thousand when this was over," he lied. "As soon as my broker feels it's the best time to sell your shares, you'll get what you're owed and more."

"Why don't I believe you, Darrell?"

"Jesus, Ruth. I've only got your best interests at heart. You're my client. We have a fiduciary relationship. Now promise me you'll stay away from the Lindstroms," Holloway said, desperate to divert Larson's attention from her money, some of which he'd lost on a bet on an NFL game he was certain he couldn't lose.

Marjorie didn't answer.

"Ruth, swear you'll forget about the baby."

The surrogate stared across the table at Holloway. Then she stood up and left the tavern.

CHAPTER FIFTEEN

Robin was in bed, staring at the ceiling, when her mother walked in. Shirley went to the window and raised the shade. Sunlight streamed into the room, and Robin turned her head away from the glare.

"It's nine thirty, Robin. Don't you think you should be up and dressed?"

"I guess," Robin said, but her response was listless.

Shirley sat on the edge of the bed. Her daughter had always been so positive and so alive, and it was very painful for Shirley to see her drained of hope and energy.

"It's sunny out, and most of the snow has melted. You should take advantage of the break in the weather and go for a run."

"I don't feel much like running, Mom."

"And I don't like seeing you turning into the Pillsbury Dough Girl. If you put on much more weight, you'll start looking like Gladys March. And what's more, a shower wouldn't hurt. You haven't showered in the two weeks you've been back, and you're starting to smell. And your hair . . ."

Shirley shook her head.

Robin reached out and placed her hand on top of her mother's hand. "I know you're trying to help, but I don't want to go for a run."

"Robin, I'm going to be blunt. You've got to stop feeling sorry for yourself. If you'd died instead of Jeff, would you have wanted him to spend the rest of his life walking around like a zombie, or would you want him to be happy?"

"You don't understand."

"Don't I? You're not the only one who's lost someone they loved more than anything. Your father and I were married forty-five years when he passed, and I still think about him every day.

"You were away in school when his heart gave out. You came back for the funeral, and I put on a happy face while you were here. That's what parents do. We don't let our children see our pain. But I can tell you that I cried myself to sleep every night for over a month, and I had crying jags when no one was around that took my breath away. So, don't tell me I don't understand grief.

"It's human to grieve, but there comes a time when you have to start moving again. I haven't said anything until now because I didn't want to intrude. But I think you've been wrapped up in sorrow long enough. And by that I don't mean you should forget Jeff or the love you had for each other. You're never going to want to do that. But I do think it's time you got your butt out of bed and started living again."

Shirley squeezed Robin's hand. Then she left.

Inspired by her champion wrestler brothers, Robin had exercised nonstop since elementary school. When she was in Portland, Robin ran five miles every weekday morning to McGill's gym, where she put herself through a grueling workout before going to her office. Robin had always been able to run for hours without pain. But she felt nothing but pain as she ran the two miles to the high school and back. Some of the pain was in her muscles, which had not been tested since the day Jeff died, but most of the pain was in her heart, and she ran in tears for a good part of her route.

Robin pulled up at the foot of the long driveway that led to her house, so she could wipe the tears from her cheeks and collect herself. When she could breathe easily and her emotions were under control, she walked up the drive.

"I'm home, Mom!" she yelled.

"I'll make breakfast while you shower."

Robin had to admit that the shower felt good. Her hair was a matted, tangled mess, and she did smell. After she dried off, Robin put on sweat socks, jeans, a long-sleeve shirt, and a sweater. The aroma of bacon wafted up from the kitchen, and she saw a plate piled high with pancakes when she walked into the kitchen.

"I thought you were worried that I'm turning into a blimp," Robin said as she sat at her place.

"I said that to motivate and shame you. A hearty breakfast is essential to good mental health."

Robin smiled. The *Elk Grove Gazette* was open on the table. Robin pulled it over while she dug into the stack of pancakes. The front page caught her eye. There was a picture of a woman named Ruth Larson and a headline that told her that Larson was a surrogate mother who was suing for custody of the baby she had carried to term for a couple named Lindstrom.

CHAPTER SIXTEEN

Darrell Holloway was furious. Ruth Larson had hired some jerk lawyer in Mill City to sue for custody of baby Roy, and she was also suing him. Darrell wasn't worried about losing; the contract Larson had signed was ironclad. What worried him was her allegation that he was selling babies. Providing surrogates had been a nice little sideline, and Darrell could see that revenue stream drying up because of the very bad publicity.

Holloway heard the front door open and close. His secretary was at lunch, so Holloway walked into the waiting room, hoping to greet a new client. Two men in business suits were standing in the waiting area. Neither of them looked like a businessman. One man looked like a biker who was wearing his suit to a costume party. The redhead could have been a bouncer at a strip club. Both men were very big and intimidating, but Holloway smiled in the hope that they were new business.

"How can I help you?"

The redhead held up a copy of the *Elk Grove Gazette* with Ruth Larson's picture on the front page. "The paper says you're Ruth Larson's lawyer."

"Yes."

"We'd like to speak with Miss Larson. We were hoping you could tell us where we can find her."

"Why do you need to speak to her?"

"It's personal."

"Miss Larson was a client, so I can't give out any information about her without her permission."

"The article says she's suing you. So, you don't owe her anything."

"I still have an obligation to keep Miss Larson's confidences." Holloway shrugged. "If I violate the ethics rules, I could be disbarred."

"We did a little digging before we came to your office, Mr. Holloway," the redhead said. "According to the State Bar, you're no stranger to complaints about ethics violations."

The other man held out an envelope. It was stuffed with cash. "We'd like to hire you to help us with our personal matter. And we can guarantee that what you tell us in an attorney-client confidential communication will never be revealed by either of us."

Holloway hesitated. Then he remembered that Larson had always been evasive when he'd asked about her past. He was certain that her story about living in Florida had been a lie and that she was running from something, but he never investigated a surrogate's background, even though he assured potential parents that he had. Investigations cost money and cut into his profits.

If these men were involved in the thing that made Ruth run, maybe she would run again if they confronted her. If she ran, he wouldn't have to worry about the money he owed her or the lawsuit.

It was pure luck that Marjorie had run out of coffee. She had just returned from the grocery store and was about to turn into the parking lot of her apartment when she spotted two huge men knocking on her door.

Marjorie drove down the block and parked where she could see her apartment. She pulled out her phone and took a picture of the men. Marjorie hoped they would leave, but it turned dark before the men drove away. Marjorie had several hours to think while she waited. As soon as she felt it was safe, she packed her bags and checked her gun to make sure it was loaded.

CHAPTER SEVENTEEN

After Emily and Caleb put Roy down for the night, Caleb put his arm around Emily's shoulder, and they stood over his crib and watched him sleep. Caleb pulled Emily to him and kissed her on the cheek. Then he took her hand and led her downstairs to the kitchen. They smiled at each other while Emily poured wine into two glasses.

"He's so beautiful," Emily said as they carried the glasses into the living room, where the couple sat on the couch and stared at the dying embers in the fireplace. They had never been so happy.

"What do you think Roy will do when he grows up?" Caleb asked.

Emily laughed. "If he's healthy and happy, I'll be satisfied."

"If he marries someone like you, he'll be a great success."

Emily reached over and squeezed Caleb's hand just as the doorbell rang.

"Who could that be at this hour?" Caleb asked. He started to stand, but Emily put her hand on his arm.

"I'll get it," she said as she walked into the entryway.

As soon as she pulled the door open, Marjorie Loman jammed the barrel of her service revolver into Emily's chest.

"Give me the baby or I'll kill you and your husband and take him anyway."

When Caleb started toward Marjorie, she hit Emily in the forehead with the gun butt. Emily grabbed her head and dropped to her knees.

"Stop or she's dead," Marjorie threatened. Caleb stopped.

"Now get the baby or I'll shoot her. Pack diapers and formula and everything I'll need to take care of Peter. I promise I won't hurt him, but I will kill you both if you do anything to keep my baby from me."

Caleb raced upstairs.

"Make it quick or she dies!" Marjorie yelled.

Moments later, Caleb came down the stairs with a carry case over his shoulder and Roy wrapped in a heavy blanket.

"Give him to Emily. Then back away," Marjorie ordered.

"Please don't hurt Roy," Emily begged as she handed over the baby.

"His name isn't Roy, it's Peter," Marjorie said as she backed out the door. "And you'd better not call the cops. I'll kill myself and my baby before I'll give him up."

Marjorie backed away, her gun aimed at Emily, who began to sob. Caleb moved to her side, and the couple watched Marjorie and their baby disappear. Emily sagged against her husband's side moments before they heard a car start, then drive away.

"Oh, God, Caleb. What are we going to do?"

"We're going to call the police."

"But she said—"

"I know what she said, but she's bluffing. She's not going to hurt Roy after all the trouble she's gone through to get him."

"She's crazy, Caleb," Emily said. "Crazy people do crazy things."

Caleb put his hands on Emily's shoulders and stared into her eyes. "Do you want to stay quiet and let an insane woman raise our child? I'm calling the sheriff."

CHAPTER EIGHTEEN

John Kaiser put down the paperback western he was reading as soon as he saw the headlights cutting through the fog in the motel parking lot. Moments later, the door to the motel office opened, and a woman walked in.

"It says you have a vacancy," she said.

Kaiser told the woman what a night's lodging would cost, and she paid in cash. He thought the woman looked familiar, but it took another half hour before he remembered where he'd seen her. The surrogate's picture had been broadcast on every local television news show in the Midwest and was displayed in most newspapers following baby Roy's kidnapping. Kaiser dialed 911.

"You know the lady who kidnapped the baby," he told the dispatcher. "She just checked into my motel."

Detective Irving Guilford and two Elk Grove police officers sped across two state lines. At three in the morning, they joined the team from the local PD that had Ruth's room under surveillance. An ambulance was parked behind the police cars.

"Seen anything?" Guilford asked after the introductions had been made.

"The lights were on when we parked," Chief Samuel Forester told Irv. "They went off about midnight. I've got a master key, so we can get in anytime you want. She didn't close the shades completely. One of my men peeked through the gap. The woman is on the bed, and the baby is sleeping on the floor on a sleeping bag. We didn't want to storm in because of the child."

"Good thinking," Guilford said. "The baby is the important thing. I have no idea whether Larson will harm the child, but I do know that she's violent and volatile. She pistol-whipped the baby's mother and kidnapped the kid at gunpoint. So, we have to assume she'll use her gun if she gets the chance."

"How do you want to proceed?" Forester asked.

"Let's use the key to get in. Then I'll take Larson, and you save the baby."

Guilford, Forester, and two deputies crossed the parking lot, and Guilford and Forester peeked through the gap between the bottom of the shade and the windowsill. Marjorie Loman was sleeping on the side of the bed farthest from the door. The baby was lying at the foot of the bed.

Guilford nodded to Forester. The police chief inserted the key and turned it slowly. As soon as he heard the lock click, he opened the door quietly. The light from the parking lot let them see the inside of the room. Guilford crept around the bed and stood over Larson. Forester grabbed the infant and raced out of the room. Guilford signaled to a deputy who had his hand on the light switch. Marjorie tried to sit up, but Guilford wrestled her onto her stomach.

"My baby!" she screamed as he cuffed her.

"Find the gun!" Guilford yelled.

"Don't hurt my baby!" Marjorie yelled.

"Your baby is safe," Guilford said. "No one is going to hurt him."

Marjorie was much smaller than Guilford, but he had to use all his strength to keep her pinned down.

"A little help!" he yelled.

One of the deputies helped drag Marjorie off the bed. Her pillow fell on the floor, revealing her service revolver. Another deputy grabbed it. A woman deputy came into the room.

"Please stop fighting," Guilford said. "You'll only hurt yourself."

"Where's Peter?" Marjorie screamed.

"He's safe. We're taking him to the hospital to make sure he's okay."

Marjorie sagged in Guilford's grip. "Please don't take my baby," she sobbed.

Roy was only wearing a diaper, and he started crying as soon as Forester carried him into the parking lot. Paramedic Arlene Castro took Roy from Chief Forester and carried the crying baby toward the ambulance. Gary Pinsky, her partner, followed.

"How's he look?" Pinsky asked.

"He's breathing on his own, but there's a large swelling on the left side of his head, and look at these bruises on his lower back."

They had just reached the ambulance when Roy started shaking.

"He's convulsing," Pinsky said.

"Let's get some Ativan in him," Castro said as she laid Roy down on a gurney.

Pinsky inserted an intravenous drip and fed Ativan through it. Castro ordered the driver to head for the hospital. Moments after they took off, the shaking stopped.

Castro looked at the pulse oximetry reading. It had been 95 percent moments before, but it was at 80 percent now.

"He's turning blue," Castro said.

"His heart rate is down to fifty-five beats per minute," Pinsky said.

Castro gave Roy 100 percent oxygen from an Ambu bag and mask, while Pinsky administered CPR with chest compressions for one minute until the heart rate was over sixty beats per minute. They continued the bag-mask breathing. When they reached the hospital, Roy's oximeter reading, cyanosis, and slow heart rate were all normal.

PART THREE

A COMPLEX CASE

DECEMBER

CHAPTER NINETEEN

Robin was up at seven on Saturday morning. Instead of staying in bed, she got ready to run. Robin had been in Elk Grove for three weeks, and she had been sad most of the time, but recently, she had started to experience a different emotion: boredom.

The day before, Loretta Washington, one of her firm's associates, had called her about a tricky issue in an appeal. The conversation had energized Robin, and she was sorry when it ended. Robin's mother, her brothers, and their families had been great, but she found herself at loose ends during the majority of each day without the challenges of her law practice to occupy her.

The upshot of all this was a feeling that her time in Elk Grove would have to end soon. Robin's client in the Getty trial had agreed to a setover, but it wasn't fair to her to put off the trial much longer. As Robin dressed for her run, she decided to start making plans to move back to Portland.

"Jack is on the phone, and he wants to know if he can run with you!" her mother yelled up to her as she was lacing up her running shoes.

"Definitely!" Robin yelled down from her room. "I was just getting ready to go."

"He'll be over in twenty minutes."

Robin smiled at the thought of running with Jack. She loved all her brothers, but her oldest brother was special. Jack, Miles, and David had all been district champs, and they'd all placed at States, but only Jack had been a state champion. Jack was also the prom king, and he had married Dana Wyse, the prom queen, a week after graduation and shortly before starting work at Anderson Meatpacking. Jack had started out on the floor, but he'd taken college classes at night and earned promotions that had boosted him into management.

Robin had asked Jack's advice before trying out for the Elk Grove High wrestling team, and Jack encouraged her. The school board told Robin she couldn't wrestle with boys after getting complaints from some of the parents. Robin's father had hired a lawyer and sued. Jack had Robin's back during the lawsuit and was instrumental in getting the coach and several wrestlers to speak up on her behalf at the hearing. Robin was convinced that Jack's support had been instrumental in winning the lawsuit and making her wrestling and MMA career possible.

"Take it easy on me," Jack begged when they started off. "The kids and married life have taken their toll."

Robin laughed. "Don't worry, old man, I know CPR. If you have a coronary, I'll keep your heart pumping until the EMTs arrive."

Robin had planned a six-mile run, and her brother hadn't complained. She didn't push the pace, and Jack didn't seem to have any trouble keeping up.

"Can you come over for dinner tonight?" Jack asked when they hit the halfway point. "Dana and the kids would love to see you."

"That sounds great. What time?"

"Five thirty. I invited Stan McDermott to join us. He graduated from law school a few years back and has his own firm in Elk Grove."

Robin stopped running. She looked furious. "I just buried Jeff, and I have absolutely no interest in being fixed up."

Her brother's jaw dropped. "Jesus, Robin, you must think I'm an insensitive asshole. This has nothing to do with a fix-up. Stan knows your reputation as a lawyer. He's got a very complicated case, and he wants to ask you about it."

Robin flushed with embarrassment. "I'm sorry. I just . . ."

"No need to apologize. I shouldn't have sprung it on you the way I did. So, will you still come?"

Dinner at Jack's was chaotic. His five-, eight-, and nine-year-olds were precocious and kept up a constant, high-pitched conversation in response to Robin's questions about school, sports, their friends, and their favorite video games. The chaos was welcome because it kept anyone from bringing up Jeff and the reason for Robin's return to Elk Grove.

As soon as dessert had been consumed, Dana and Jack took the children upstairs to change into their pajamas and get ready for bed, leaving Robin and Stan in the living room with cups of freshly brewed coffee.

Stan McDermott was an inch shorter than Robin, with curly black hair, gentle blue eyes, and an easy smile. She thought he looked handsome and fit, and she was certain she recognized him.

"Were you on the wrestling team with Jack that won States his senior year?"

"I was," Stan admitted.

"You were our one-hundred-and-twenty-two pounder."

"A weight class you represented with distinction a few years later," Stan said with an impish grin.

"Not as well as you. If I remember correctly, you and Jack were our state champs, and you went undefeated."

Stan smiled. "That team was loaded. Jack and I placed first, but the team won because we had one second- and two third-placers."

"Didn't you wrestle after high school?"

Stan nodded. "I got a scholarship to Iowa State."

"How'd you do?"

"It was an up-and-down career. I placed sixth at the NCAAs as a freshman, but that was the high point. I blew out my knee at the beginning of my sophomore year. When I came back as a junior, the coach had recruited a hotshot frosh who'd been a state champ in Indiana. I never beat him. I did win a few matches at a different weight, and I placed fourth at the Midlands, but I burned out and quit in my senior year to concentrate on getting my grades up for law school."

"Where did you go?"

"I came back home and went to State. Then I hung out a shingle in Elk Grove. I have a small firm with two associates. We take anything that comes in the door—wills, divorces, some personal injury, and a smattering of criminal cases—but I enjoy being part of the community."

"Jack said you wanted to talk to me about a case."

"I do. I've handled one manslaughter and a vehicular homicide along with less serious criminal cases, but

I'm not sure I have the experience to handle a case as complex as this one, and I'd appreciate your advice."

Robin yawned, and Stan smiled. "It's getting late, and you look tired. There's a lot you need to know before you can give me a well-informed opinion. Would you be up for breakfast at Lee's at nine tomorrow?"

Robin grinned. "I am always up for breakfast at Lee's."

"Okay, then. And it's on me. Consider it a consulting fee."

Before Robin could say anything else, Jack and Dana joined them, and the next half hour was taken up with trivial conversation, which was just fine with Robin.

The evening broke up at nine thirty, and Robin went to bed as soon as she got home, but she didn't fall asleep right away. She couldn't stop wondering about Stan's case.

Robin decided that she liked Stan. He had admitted that he might not be able to handle his case, which showed an admirable lack of ego, something that male attorneys did not often demonstrate. And he was good-looking and . . .

The minute she thought about Stan's looks, Robin was overwhelmed by guilt. How could she think about a man in that way with Jeff dead? She remembered how mad she'd gotten at Jack when she thought he was trying to fix her up, and here she was thinking about the lawyer's looks, like a high school girl after a first date.

Robin got out of bed and went to the window. She pulled up the shade and looked out at the field behind the house. There was enough moonlight to see the swing set Shirley had erected for the grandkids and the silhouette of the trees that formed the field's far border.

Robin felt tears forming and wiped at her eyes.

"I love you so much, Jeff," she whispered.

Robin was not religious, and she did not believe in heaven or an afterlife, but no one could know for sure what happened when you died, so she told Jeff that she hoped he was somewhere safe and warm.

Crying exhausted Robin, and she stumbled back to bed, still feeling bad when fatigue dragged her into a troubled sleep.

CHAPTER TWENTY

Lee's was on Main Street opposite the town square, and it was Elk Grove's most popular restaurant. Frank Lee, Andy Lee's father, had opened the place in the 1950s, and Andy met his wife, Sophie, when they worked at the restaurant as a cook and waitress during the summer to earn money for college. When Frank retired, Andy inherited Lee's.

Andy had wrestled for Elk Grove and was a huge supporter of the team. Robin had fond memories of the free pizzas the Lees gave the wrestling team after each home match. Most of the wall space in the dining room was taken up by pictures of victorious Elk Grove athletes grouped by their sport, but there were also pictures of Lee's early days and the occasional politician or celebrity who had dined at the restaurant.

Sophie Lee was a large woman who greeted customers at a stand by the entrance with a smile as wide as her waistline. She had been Robin's biggest fan when Robin became the first girl to wrestle for the Elk Grove team, and Robin's picture was prominently displayed on the restaurant's wall alongside Elk Grove's team and individual state wrestling champions.

When Robin walked in, Sophie wrapped her up in an energetic hug and pulled her into her massive breasts.

"How are you doing, honey?" Sophie asked with genuine concern when she'd released Robin.

"Not great," Robin answered.

"Oh, baby," Sophie said. "I heard what happened, and I'm so sorry."

"Thanks."

"If I remember, the Farmer's Special was always your favorite."

"Only after the season, when I didn't have to pull weight."

Sophie studied Robin. "You're not wrestling anymore, so the Farmer's or anything else you order is on the house."

"Actually, Sophie, I'm meeting Stan McDermott, and he's picking up the tab."

Sophie looked surprised, and Robin turned red when it dawned on her that Sophie might think she was on a date.

"It's business. He wants to talk to me about a case."

Now it was Sophie's turn to be embarrassed. "The one with the surrogate?"

"I don't know yet. Is Stan here?"

"I just seated him. He's in a booth in the back. Tell him you're both eating for free and not to be shy about what you order."

"In that case, we'll have your most expensive champagne and a tub of beluga caviar."

Sophie's hearty laugh trailed Robin as she dodged around the crowded tables. Some of Lee's customers couldn't help staring at Robin because she was a local celebrity. In her first year of law school, Robin fought in televised, pay-per-view MMA matches and was known nationwide as "Rockin' Robin." Recently, the tragic death of her fiancé had been front-page news in the *Elk Grove Gazette*.

Stan saw Robin and waved. Robin waved back.

"Sophie says that breakfast is on the house," Robin told Stan.

"Damn, I already ordered oatmeal."

"'At Lee's, where calories don't count'?" Robin said, quoting the restaurant's motto. "You're not thinking of pulling weight, so you can make a comeback, are you?"

Stan laughed. "I'm just not into a heavy breakfast

this morning, but don't let me stop you from pigging out."

Robin didn't, and she ordered the Farmer's Special.

"So, tell me about your case," Robin said as soon as the waitress filled her cup with coffee and left with her order.

"I've been hired by a woman who came to Elk Grove using the name Ruth Larson. When she was arrested, they ran her prints. Her real name is Marjorie Loman, and she's a police officer in Profit, Oregon—your neck of the woods—who went missing shortly after Joel Loman, her husband, was murdered."

"The plot thickens."

"Indeed, it does. I'm involved because Caleb and Emily Lindstrom couldn't have children, so they hired a local attorney named Darrell Holloway, who told them about surrogacy. Do you know what that is?"

Robin nodded.

"Holloway met Marjorie soon after she came to town. She needed money, and Holloway told her that she would be paid to bring the Lindstroms' baby to term. Marjorie accepted, and she gave birth to a baby boy in October. That's when the trouble started.

"The hospital had dealt with surrogates before, and there were explicit instructions in Marjorie's chart that she was not to have any contact with the baby after she gave birth, but that monster storm hit Elk Grove the night Marjorie gave birth."

"I remember. It was something."

"Yeah. Power lines were down, the roads were a mess, and due to the chaos caused by the storm, the Lindstroms were never notified that Marjorie was in labor.

"Marjorie was rushed to the hospital during the worst part of the storm. The delivery took a long time, and from what I've learned, it was an ordeal. The nurse who helped with the delivery never saw the note about the surrogacy, and she brought the baby to Marjorie's room. Marjorie breastfed the baby and spent the night with him before the hospital became aware of the problem. They gave the baby to the Lindstroms the next morning. By then, the damage had been done."

"Marjorie bonded with the baby?"

Stan nodded. "Marjorie went downhill very quickly after they took the baby from her. She has all the symptoms of postpartum depression. She also believes that there was a conspiracy to steal her baby that included her lawyer, the Lindstroms, the hospital, and a host of other coconspirators.

"One evening, Marjorie showed up at the Lindstroms and demanded the child. They refused. Shortly after, Marjorie kidnapped the baby and went on the run. Her picture was plastered over every newspaper in the Midwest and broadcast on every television news show. Marjorie evaded capture until a motel clerk recognized her when she checked in. He called the police, and Marjorie was arrested."

"Was the baby with her?"

"Yes, and he's okay, but there is a problem. At the motel, the baby was given to two paramedics who took him to the hospital. They say that Roy had convulsions at the scene and other medical problems. The emergency room doctor who examined Roy noted extensive bruising on his lower back and buttocks, swelling on the left side of his head, retinal hemorrhages, and other indications of abuse. She told Rodney Hatcher that Marjorie must have shaken the baby violently to cause the injuries."

"Who is Rodney Hatcher?"

"He's our county prosecutor. He's young, ambitious, and very sharp."

"How much trouble is your client in?"

"She's been charged with assaulting the baby and Emily Lindstrom, and kidnapping the baby. Hatcher is going to trial using the shaken baby syndrome to prove his case about the assault on Roy Lindstrom. Do you know anything about the syndrome?"

"I attended an Oregon Criminal Defense Lawyers Association seminar a few years ago where a speaker raised questions about its scientific foundation," Robin said. "I'll call my office and have copies of the materials from the seminar sent to your office."

"Thanks."

"Why was Marjorie using an alias in Elk Grove?"

"Marjorie was in the middle of a nasty divorce when her husband was tortured and murdered. Before he was killed, Joel looted the couple's accounts, embezzled money from his investment firm, and hid millions of dollars. No one knows where the money is.

"Marjorie claims that two men showed up at her house in Oregon and said Joel owed their employer a quarter of a million dollars. Marjorie said that they implied that they had murdered Joel and would kill her if she didn't make good on his debt. She says that she fled to Elk Grove and used a phony name because she was afraid of the men. She also claims that she saw these men in Elk Grove on the day she took the baby. Marjorie says that she ran with the baby to escape from them."

"Are the men still in Elk Grove?"

"She gave me a description, and we haven't been able to find anyone who matches it."

"Is Marjorie out on bail?"

"No. Hatcher argued that she's a flight risk, and there's a warrant from Portland for her arrest on a murder charge."

"Is the victim the husband?"

Stan nodded. "I'll need to know about that case because I'm sure Hatcher will try to tell the jury about it."

"I can have one of my associates check up on it."

"Thanks," Stan said just as their waitress placed a bowl of oatmeal in front of him and put a plate covered with eggs, bacon, hash browns, and biscuits in front of Robin.

Stan shook his head. "I'm glad we got to talk before you passed away from a cholesterol overdose."

"I have a very active metabolism, and I'm very hungry."

"I'm also glad Sophie is footing the bill on this. I don't think I've earned enough money this month to cover your tab."

Robin smiled and instantly felt guilty for having fun when Jeff was dead.

Stan noticed the sudden change in Robin's expression. "Are you okay?" he asked.

"Yeah, I'm fine. Is there anything else I should know about the case?" she asked.

"I think that's enough for now. I would be very grateful if you told me anything you think of that might help my defense. I can give you the discovery I've received if you want to look at it."

"Send it to my mom's place."

"Uhm, there's one other thing."

"Yes?"

"You've got way more experience than I do with complex criminal cases, and I was wondering if you'd be interested in cocounseling with me? Marjorie owned property in Oregon. She gave her lawyer power of attorney before she left, and he sold it, so she can pay you."

Robin was going to turn Stan down, but she hesitated. She had a thing about junk science that made the shaken baby aspect of special interest.

"When are you scheduled to go to trial?"

"It's set for a month from now."

"Phew. That's cutting it close."

"I can ask for a new trial date."

"I don't know, Stan. I was thinking about going back to Portland soon."

McDermott couldn't hide his disappointment. "I get that. You have your own firm."

"Why don't you send me the discovery and let me think about your offer."

Stan brightened. "I'll have someone bring copies to your house tomorrow."

"I'll give you an answer soon. I won't keep you hanging."

"I appreciate that."

Stan wanted to ask Robin how she was coping with her tragedy, but he knew that would be the wrong thing to do, so he pointed his spoon at Robin's plate. "Your food is getting cold."

Robin smiled and shook salt and pepper on the yolks of her sunny-side-up eggs. Then she dug in.

"This is as good as I remember," she said after swallowing a mouthful.

"I've never had a bad meal at Lee's."

"So, how is the team doing this year?" Robin asked, steering the conversation onto a safe topic.

CHAPTER TWENTY-ONE

The next morning, a messenger delivered copies of the discovery in Marjorie Loman's case. When Robin finished with the police reports, medical reports, and crime lab reports, she went for a run, because that's when she did some of her best thinking.

It was cold but sunny, and the fresh air cleared away the cobwebs that had formed while she was reading the discovery. The doctor who had examined the baby was convinced that Marjorie had assaulted the child. They would have to consult an expert to see if there was an alternative explanation for the injuries.

The kidnapping charge looked open and shut, but Marjorie's behavior had been odd after she gave birth, and that had given Robin an idea. It was a weird idea, but she would mention it to Stan. Robin didn't know if anyone had ever raised a defense like it before, but one of her strengths was attacking difficult problems with novel approaches.

By the time Robin finished her run, she was very excited about challenging the shaken baby syndrome and the possibility of raising an innovative defense to the kidnapping charge, but she foresaw an obstacle to doing this successfully. For the defenses Robin had envisioned to work, Marjorie Loman had to be believable.

The Elk Grove Courthouse was two blocks west of the town square. The three-story brick building had been erected in 1927 after a fire destroyed the wooden building that had housed the court since the late 1800s. The courthouse's design was unbalanced by a massive clock tower that stood on the far-left side of the roof. Every time Robin saw the tower, she had an unsettling feeling that it might pull the entire building over at any minute.

Until the 1950s, the jail consisted of six cells on the top floor above the courtrooms. In 1956, a bond measure had provided the funds for a modern annex that housed the sheriff's department and an expanded jail facility. Soon after Robin met Stan in the waiting area, a corrections officer escorted them to an interview room. Moments later, a matron led their client into the room.

Marjorie Loman looked utterly defeated. She had stopped dyeing her hair, and the natural blond color now had the unkempt appearance of brownish-yellow dishwater. She sagged inside a rumpled blue jumpsuit, and she slouched when she walked toward the lawyers with her shoulders folded inward and her eyes on the floor. When she did look up, Robin saw dark circles under her eyes that spoke of sleepless nights and fatigue-filled days.

"Marjorie, this is Robin Lockwood," Stan said when the matron left. "She's an Oregon attorney who grew up in Elk Grove. She's been visiting her family and has been kind enough to consult on your case."

Marjorie studied Robin for a moment. "I've heard of you. You're a big-shot criminal defense attorney in Portland."

Robin smiled. "My office is in Portland, but I'm not sure how big a shot I am."

Marjorie didn't return the smile. Instead, she began to sob. "You can't help me. I've made a mess of my life. There are too many powerful people who don't want me to have my baby. They'll make sure I go to prison."

Robin was grieving too, and she sensed that Marjorie's grief was genuine.

"Hey," Robin said as she reached across the table and laid a comforting hand on top of her new client's. "You have every reason to be sad. Everyone gets depressed when they're put in a cell. But it's too early to give up hope."

"They say I hurt my baby," she sobbed. "I would never hurt Peter."

Robin made a mental note of the fact that Marjorie had called the baby Peter when his name was Roy.

"The district attorney has a doctor who believes in a theory about how babies can be injured when there are no external signs of abuse," Robin said. "But there are other doctors who have serious reservations about the theory. Stan is going to talk to those experts about your case. He's not promising anything, but depending on what they say, he might convince the jurors to have a reasonable doubt about whether you injured Peter."

Marjorie shook her head. "It won't matter. They'll make sure I'm locked away, so those people can keep my baby."

Robin frowned. "Who do you think is trying to keep you from Peter?"

"The Lindstroms, the nurses, and the doctors at the hospital. They control the police. They'll make sure I never get out."

"Don't give up hope, Marjorie. Stan is a very good lawyer."

Marjorie didn't respond, so Robin moved on. "I'd like to ask you a few questions. Some of them will be questions other people have asked you, but I'm new to your case, and I want to hear what you have to say. Would that be okay?"

Marjorie nodded.

"How did you feel after you gave birth?"

"I was exhausted. It was long and painful, and all I wanted to do was sleep."

"I understand that a nurse brought Peter to your room in the hospital. How did that make you feel?"

Marjorie smiled. "At first, I didn't want him. I just wanted to rest. But the nurse laid him on my chest, and he felt so warm and soft and . . ."

Marjorie started to sob again. "When I woke up in the morning, he was gone. They'd taken my baby."

"Didn't you expect that? You knew the baby would go to the Lindstroms."

"If I'd known how much I wanted Peter, I wouldn't have signed the contract."

"But you did."

"And it ate me alive. I couldn't sleep, I couldn't eat. I just wanted my baby."

"How were you feeling when you went to the Lindstroms?"

"I'd seen the men. I was afraid they would kill me."

"What men?" Robin asked even though Stan had told her about them.

"I was married, and my husband was murdered in Portland. After he died, two men came to my house. They said they'd killed and tortured Joel and they'd do the same to me if I didn't give them the quarter of a million dollars that they claimed Joel owed them.

"Joel and I were going through a bad divorce. He'd cleaned out our bank accounts and hidden our money somewhere. I didn't have a quarter of a million dollars. I barely had enough money to get by. I ran away to Elk Grove to escape those men. When I saw them here, I knew I had to run again."

"Where did you see them?"

"Outside my apartment. I was coming back from the grocery store, and they were watching it. When they left, I packed up and ran."

"You could have left without Peter. Weren't you afraid he'd be in danger if the men found you?"

"I wasn't thinking straight. I knew I'd never see Peter again if I left without him, so I . . ." She shook her head. "That night is a blur. I don't even remember everything I did. They say I hit Emily and threatened to . . . to shoot her. I know that happened, but . . ." She shook her head again.

Robin could see how upset Marjorie was, and she didn't want to cause her more distress. Besides, she'd gotten what she'd come for.

"I have one more question before we go. Why, of all the towns in America, did you move to Elk Grove?"

Marjorie's brow furrowed as she sought the answer to Robin's question. Then it smoothed out, and she started to laugh.

"What's so funny?" Robin asked.

"I just remembered. It was my sandwich."

"Pardon?"

Marjorie smiled. "I made myself a ham sandwich for lunch, and the meat was from Anderson Meatpacking. The package said they were in Elk Grove, so that's where I decided to go."

Stan and Robin talked to Marjorie for fifteen minutes more before leaving. When they were outside, Robin turned to Stan.

"That poor woman. She's in so much pain."

"Losing the baby is killing her," Stan agreed.

"I'd like to help you with the case, but I have to check with my partner in Portland to see if my being gone for an extended period is going to be a problem."

"I'll understand if you can't stay here for the trial. I feel we'd have a fighting chance with you at the counsel table, but you do what's best for your firm."

"Thanks, Stan. I want to help. I don't know if we'd win. The odds are stacked against us. But I feel really bad for Marjorie."

Robin called her partner, Mark Berman, as soon as she left Stan. Mark was in his early thirties, married, and the proud father of a daughter who had just started preschool. He had thick brown hair, brown eyes, and a rugged physique that was the result of years of competitive crew.

"Hi, Mark," she said when her partner took her call. "How are things in the big city?"

"Same old, same old. It's raining, overcast, and dreary. How's the weather where you are?"

"Cold and snowy. Has my being gone caused problems?"

"Nah. We've decided you're not that important."

Robin laughed.

"We do miss you, though. There's no one here to blame for the screwups."

"You can relax, then. I'm flying back this week."

"You're sure you're ready?"

"Yeah. Mom and my brothers have been great, and the change of scenery helped, but I'm going to be sad whether I'm in Portland or Elk Grove."

"It would be weird if you weren't."

Robin started to choke up. She knew she would start bawling if she didn't do something fast, so she switched the subject to Marjorie Loman's case.

"I might be returning to Elk Grove soon after I get to Portland."

"Oh?"

"Stan McDermott, a local lawyer, wants me to cocounsel a very interesting case. It's retained, and there's a decent fee. The trial starts in a few weeks, so I'd be away again until it's over. Is that okay? Because I can turn him down if it's going to cause too many problems in Portland."

"What makes the case so interesting?" Mark asked.

"Do you know what a surrogate mother is?"

"Yes."

"The defendant is a surrogate mother who kidnapped a baby after she gave birth and the legal parents had custody. The police were tipped off that the mother was holed up at a motel with the baby. They raided the motel and took the kid to a hospital. The doctor who treated the baby says the baby was abused. There are no signs of the type of external injuries you'd expect given the internal injuries she claims to have found. The prosecutor is using the shaken baby syndrome to explain how that's possible."

"Didn't you learn about the syndrome at that conference on the coast?"

"Yeah. There's a lot of controversy about it. One reason I'm calling is to have you send a copy of the materials from the seminar to Elk Grove."

"I'll overnight them."

"If I cocounsel the case, I'd be handling the expert witnesses. I can prep for the experts from our office and work on my other cases while I'm in town."

"I don't see a problem with you taking on the case in Elk Grove. The Getty trial is set for March, so you have breathing room there, and Loretta had done drafts in your appeals."

"One more thing. The defendant is a woman named Marjorie Loman. She's from Profit, Oregon. Her husband, Joel Loman, was murdered in Portland shortly before she moved to Elk Grove. Stan says that she's been indicted in Oregon for her husband's murder. Can you have Loretta find out about the case and send me the info?"

"Of course."

"Okay. I'll tell Stan I'll cocounsel."

"When are you flying back?" Mark asked. "I can meet you at the airport."

Robin gave Mark the date and her flight information.

"It will be great having you around. We're all thinking of you."

"I know, and it helps. See you soon."

CHAPTER TWENTY-TWO

Mark Berman picked up Robin at the airport at ten at night and drove her to her apartment. He offered to go up with her, but it was late, and she told him she'd be okay. But she wasn't.

Robin hesitated before opening the door. The apartment had always been a warm place filled with love and laughter, but the last time she'd been there was on the day after Jeff's funeral, and it had been the saddest place she'd ever known.

Robin walked into the living room and stood at the window in the dark, looking out over the low-rise buildings on the east side of the Willamette River. On the western shore, lights illuminated the high-rise office buildings that made up Portland's skyline. Robin remembered all the times she'd been enchanted by the same scene while holding hands with Jeff.

Robin turned from the window and fought to keep from crying. She lost the battle and collapsed on the nearest chair. Her chest heaved, and she squeezed her eyes tightly shut. When the crying stopped, she made a decision. She would look for a new place to live. The apartment was too full of ghosts.

Robin slept fitfully. When she woke up, she couldn't wait to get away from her apartment. She got into her workout gear as fast as she could and set off on the five-mile run to McGill's gym.

Barry McGill was a crusty old man with the manners of a pre-self-esteem-era football coach. He had boxed professionally and had the flattened nose and scar tissue to prove it. McGill had been at the funeral, and Robin dreaded the possibility of a mushy, sentimental reunion when she reentered the gym. She needn't have worried.

"It's about time you got back to work," McGill growled. "Your buddy Martinez has been in regular, and she's been working out for a half hour already. Don't expect any sympathy if she kicks your sorry ass."

Robin was relieved that Barry was sensitive enough to treat her as if nothing had happened.

Sally Martinez, a CPA who'd been an All-American wrestler at Pacific University and had studied mixed martial arts, was a frequent sparring partner for Robin. Robin was a shade better than her friend, but Martinez always gave her a hard time. Sally had sent flowers to Jeff's grave and had attended Jeff's funeral.

"How are you doing?" Sally asked when Robin drew near.

"Better."

"Are you back for good?"

"Pretty much. I'm cocounseling a case in my hometown in a few weeks, so I'll be there for the trial. But I'm going into the office starting today."

"Did you work out while you were away?"

"I ran and joined a gym, but I just pumped iron and hit the heavy bag. No sparring."

Martinez grinned. "Good. I plan to take full advantage of your lack of training."

Robin returned the grin and shifted into a fighting stance.

Sally showed no mercy, and Robin was beaten up and winded when she called it quits. Even though she hurt, Robin was glad she had been able to lose herself in combat, where she was forced to maintain focus and was free of thoughts of her personal tragedy.

Robin kept a suit at McGill's to wear to the office after she worked out. She had forgotten to get it after the shooting, but she remembered it was in her locker before she left her apartment. Robin showered and dressed, then picked up a latte and a scone on the way to her office.

On her first day back, everyone but Mark walked on eggshells when they were around Robin, unsure of the right thing to say. That made Robin uncomfortable, and she spent the morning with her door closed sorting through snail mail and emails, a welcome distraction.

Robin left for lunch at noon. After a quick bite at her favorite sushi restaurant, she met Lori Kim, a former client who worked in real estate. Robin had phoned her shortly after arriving at her office and told Lori what she was looking for. Lori had a list of condos and apartments that fit the description.

When Robin moved to Portland to start her job with Regina Barrister, her choice of apartments was limited by her associate's salary, but she was a partner in the firm now, and the firm was doing well enough for her to look at more upscale digs. By midafternoon, she had chosen a condo on the west side of the Willamette within easy walking distance from her office. The feature Robin treasured the most was the view of the mountains and the river, which was completely different from the view she had from her apartment—a view that would always remind her of Jeff.

Robin knew that she would miss the bohemian feel of her neighborhood with its restaurants, art galleries, and mom-and-pop shops, but she needed to have a place where Jeff had never been to ease her pain.

After Lori left her, Robin called her office and told Mark she was going home. When she walked into the apartment, her chest seized up. Robin collapsed on the couch and saw Jeff seated across from her. The apparition wavered like a hologram in a science fiction movie.

"I'm so sorry," Robin told Jeff between sobs, "but I can't stay here. When I'm in this room or our bed, I miss you so much."

Jeff smiled. In her mind, Robin heard him say it was all right. Robin doubled over. Tears poured down her cheeks.

After a while, her breathing returned to normal. Crying had exhausted her. She closed her eyes and rested her head on the back of the couch. Where, she asked herself, would Jeff's spirit go when she moved? Would it be trapped here, haunting the apartment forever?

Robin decided that the thing that made Jeff special

wasn't his body. It was something that you could not see or touch that made him unique. You could call it a soul or a spirit. The name didn't matter. And that part of Jeff would always be with her.

CHAPTER TWENTY-THREE

Living in her condo was very different from living in her apartment. The tenants in the other apartments where she and Jeff had lived were students or young professionals who were just starting out. The tenants in her condo were partners in large law firms, politicians, and successful entrepreneurs. If Robin had moved into the condo straight out of Elk Grove or after graduating from her state university, she would have felt out of place, but Robin had hobnobbed with the rich and powerful at Yale, and she'd been a celebrity who'd met famous athletes and actors during her MMA career.

Robin's apartment had been furnished when she rented it. Before she moved, she sold or gave away everything she and Jeff had added to it, because she could not bear to see the dishes or artwork that would be a painful reminder of the life they had shared. Robin did keep every photo and video of Jeff, because she was terrified of forgetting what he looked and sounded like.

Two weeks after returning to Portland, Robin entered her new residence with take-out sushi. She'd started furnishing the place, and she sat on a sofa in the living room and watched the mountains of the Cascade Range disappear as the sun set.

When Robin finished eating, she started to phone Stan McDermott. Then she hesitated. Elk Grove was in a different time zone from Portland, and it would be two hours later there. Robin knew that Stan was single, but she didn't know if he had a girlfriend, and she wondered if she'd be interrupting something she shouldn't if she called this late. Then she decided that she was being stupid and she made the call.

"Hi, Stan, it's Robin. Is this a good time? I know it's late there."

"This is an excellent time. I'm all by my lonesome, nursing a beer and deciding which of two movies I want to watch. What's up?"

"I've lined up two experts. I emailed you their phone numbers, emails, and curricula vitae, so you can talk to them and decide if you want them as witnesses."

"If you picked them, I'm sure they're great."

"Dr. Gabrielle Suarez is the psychiatrist I talked to

about a postpartum depression defense. She wants to interview Marjorie before she gives a diagnosis, so you need to arrange that. We'll have to wait on Suarez, but she might really help with the kidnapping charge.

"Dr. Maxwell Lancaster has read over the medical stuff, and he disagrees with the State's medical expert."

"Thanks, Robin. This sounds terrific."

"Okay. Well, I'll let you get back to deciding what movie you want to watch."

"It will be a challenge." McDermott paused for a second. Then he asked, "How are you doing?"

Robin took a breath. "Thanks for asking. I'm doing okay. Not great, but much better than when I left Portland for Elk Grove."

"I'm glad to hear that."

Stan was miles away, and that made it easier to talk.

"I moved," Robin confided. "I just couldn't stay in the apartment where Jeff and I lived. I found a condo with a great view. I'm sitting in my living room now watching Mount Hood disappear while I eat my dinner."

Stan could hear the sadness in Robin's voice, and he switched to a safe subject.

"What's for dinner?"

"Sushi."

"Ugh, raw fish. I don't know how you preppy types can eat that stuff."

"I think a meat-eating savage like you would like sushi if you gave it a shot."

"Going to Yale and living in Portland has definitely fucked you up, Robin."

Robin laughed. "Go back to your beer and movie. I'm betting it's some macho action flick and not an intellectual, subtitled French film."

"I'm fluent in French, you snob," Stan said in perfect French.

"Well, aren't you full of surprises," Robin answered in her so-so French.

Stan laughed. "I'll call those experts tomorrow. See you soon."

The call ended, but Robin still held her phone. Stan's ability to speak French with a perfect accent had surprised her, and she realized that she knew very little about her cocounsel.

PART FOUR

THE SHAKEN BABY

JANUARY

CHAPTER TWENTY-FOUR

Pro hac vice is a Latin term that means "for the occasion or event," and this motion is made on behalf of an attorney who is not admitted to the bar in a particular jurisdiction who wants to participate in a specific case. In late January, Robin moved back to Elk Grove. The next day, Stan McDermott brought her to the courthouse, so he could make a *pro hac vice* motion on her behalf.

Robin was used to trying cases in the state and federal courthouses in Portland, where marble Corinthian columns, high ceilings, ornate molding, polished wood daises, and the latest in high-tech innovations were the norm. The courtroom where Marjorie Loman was going to be tried had no frills, and the only decorations were the state and American flags that stood on either side of the dais where the judge sat and fading oil paintings of judges past that hung on walls in need of fresh paint.

The courtroom was half filled with lawyers, clients, and retirees who watched the proceedings for entertainment. Waiting inside the bar of the court was Rodney Hatcher, the thirty-two-year-old county prosecutor. Hatcher was a handsome man made more photogenic by a professionally coiffed hairdo, manicured nails, and a hand-tailored suit. Stan had told Robin that being elected as the youngest county prosecutor in Elk Grove history was only the beginning of Hatcher's political ambitions. The prosecutor had married into local royalty when he wed Alice Anderson of the meatpacking Andersons. The political influence of the Anderson clan wasn't limited to Elk Grove. It stretched across the state and into the centers of power in Washington, D.C.

Hatcher turned when he heard the door to the courtroom open. "I see you've brought in the big guns, Stanley," he said.

"Robin, this gentleman is Rodney Hatcher, our esteemed county prosecutor. Rodney, this is Robin Lockwood, my cocounsel."

"No need to introduce the young lady. Her fame precedes her. I don't usually watch cage fights, but everyone in Elk Grove used to tune in when you were on a card."

"My UFC career has been over for a long time," Robin said.

"It's still big news here, and I'm afraid I'll have to ask potential jurors if your celebrity will have an undue influence on them."

Stan started to say something when the door to the judge's chambers opened and the Honorable Mitchell Stonehouse took the bench. Stonehouse, a skinny, bald septuagenarian with wrinkled skin and watery eyes, was as plain as his judicial domain. Stan had briefed Robin on the judge. The good news was that he treated attorneys with respect as long as they were on time and didn't engage in any shenanigans. The bad news was that Stonehouse had a short attention span and was bored by the complex legal arguments a Yale graduate and former Oregon Supreme Court clerk might make. Stan's advice was to make any points in twenty-five words or less and with as few multisyllable words as possible.

Stan had arranged to have his motion lead the docket, and the bailiff called the case as soon as Judge Stonehouse was seated.

"Good morning, Mr. McDermott," Stonehouse said. "I see we're here on your motion to have Miss Lockwood admitted *pro hac vice* for the Loman trial."

"Yes, Your Honor. Miss Lockwood grew up in Elk Grove, her family is here, and she consulted with me on various complex aspects of the case during a recent visit. She's a member in good standing of the Oregon and Federal Bars, and she would provide valuable assistance to Mrs. Loman if you permit her to be a member of the defense team."

"Any objection, Mr. Hatcher?"

"No, Your Honor."

"Then the motion is granted. Anything further?"

"No, Your Honor," Hatcher and McDermott said.

"Then let's hear the next case."

"Hatcher seems pleasant enough," Robin said when she and Stan were in the hall outside the courtroom.

"Don't be fooled by his charming manner. Rodney Hatcher is very egotistical and can be quite ruthless. He never came out and said it, but he's made it clear to me in several subtle ways that he resents the fact that I'm bringing in an out-of-state, big-city lawyer on Marjorie's case."

Robin laughed. "I lived much longer in Elk Grove than I have in Portland."

"Sorry, Robin. That doesn't count anymore now that you've deserted your roots and become a sushi-eating, Ivy League liberal."

CHAPTER TWENTY-FIVE

Robin settled into a routine during her first week back in Elk Grove. Every morning, she would go for a long run, eat a hearty breakfast, and show up at the law firm when it opened at eight o'clock. The law office was a few blocks from the courthouse in a converted Victorian mansion. A marriage counselor had offices on the second floor, an accounting firm had offices on the top floor, and the law firm took up the bottom floor. Stan had set up an office for Robin in an empty room toward the back of the building.

Robin and Stan had agreed on a division of labor. Stan would handle the opening statement and the closing argument, the cross-examination of the State's nonexpert witnesses, and the direct examination of Marjorie's nonexpert witnesses. Robin would write the defense jury instructions, write and argue any legal motions, cross-examine the State's experts, and conduct the direct examination of Marjorie's experts. Stan's two associates, Marla Peterson and Ray Flores, were available to help the defense team.

On Wednesday, Stan was in court until four thirty. When he returned, he went to Robin's office, and they reviewed the jury instructions Robin had put together.

"I've drafted a motion in limine to keep out any mention of Joel's murder," Robin said when they'd put the jury instructions aside.

"Good. We definitely don't want the jury knowing that Marjorie fled to Elk Grove right after her husband was killed."

Stan looked at his watch. "It's a little after seven, and I'm famished. Are you up for dinner?"

"Sounds good," Robin answered as she collected her papers. "Where are you thinking?"

"We don't have any foreign raw-fish restaurants in Elk Grove," Stan said with a grin, "but Buster's serves good American food if you're up for a steak, and Canton Village has decent Chinese."

"Let's do Buster's. I'm afraid someone with your narrow provincial mind will conclude that I'm a communist if I opt for Chinese."

Stan and Robin talked about the expert testimony during the walk to Buster's and continued the discussion over beers, pausing the conversation when the waitress brought their steaks, baked potatoes, salads, and sweet corn.

"Where did you learn to speak French?" Robin asked when she came up for air.

"I spent a year at the Sorbonne between college and law school."

"Wow. So, you're not the unsophisticated hick you appear to be."

Stan grinned. "I can be a hick and still speak fluent French."

"Why the Sorbonne?"

"Probably for the same reason you went to Yale. I wanted to see what life was like outside of Elk Grove, and Iowa State wasn't a whole lot different. There were some very bright people there, including some of the wrestlers, but it was still the Midwest and there wasn't much diversity.

"I'd taken French in high school, and I minored in it in college, so studying in France made a lot of sense. Not that I did a lot of studying. I used the year to travel all over Europe, and I even fit in Russia and a few weeks in the Middle East before heading back home for law school."

"Why did you go to State for law school? I'm guessing you had pretty good grades, and the year at the Sorbonne would have looked great on your law school application."

"Part of it was money, which I and my family didn't

have. I was accepted at two top-ten law schools, but they cost an arm and a leg. State gave me a full ride. But that wasn't the deciding factor. I love Elk Grove, and I always wanted to practice here, which made going local a smart move. The contacts I made staying close to home for law school have really helped my practice."

"That makes sense," Robin said.

"Did you ever think of practicing here?"

Robin shook her head. "I couldn't wait to get away. I'm not crazy about Elk Grove. I never really fit in, and I really resented the community trying to keep me from wrestling just because I was a girl."

"Yale is about as far from Elk Grove as you could go," Stan said.

"That it was."

"You must have been top of your class and blown out the LSATs to get in."

Robin laughed. "My college grades and law boards were pretty good, but I suspect being an MMA television celebrity in college had a lot to do with it."

Stan was about to say that he was glad Robin had decided to spend some time in Elk Grove when he remembered why she'd returned. So, he asked her about her time at Yale, her MMA career, and her most interesting cases and steered away from anything that touched on Robin's tragedy.

"Can I give you a lift home?" Stan asked when they were finished with dinner.

"That would be great," Robin said. "I can barely move after this meal."

Stan's car was parked in front of the law office. As they walked the three blocks from the restaurant, it dawned on Robin that she had not thought about Jeff during dinner. That made Robin uneasy, and her unease increased when she got in Stan's car. Being with Stan in the dark in his car seemed like a date, even though it definitely was not. Stan must have sensed that Robin was nervous because she noticed that he stared straight ahead and didn't talk to her during the trip to Shirley's house.

Robin jumped out as soon as Stan parked in front. "Thanks for the ride," she managed.

"See you tomorrow," Stan said.

Shirley was watching television and asked Robin if she wanted to join her. Robin said that she was beat and hurried to her room. As soon as Robin closed her door, she lay down on her bed. She was an emotional mess. She liked Stan, and she hated the fact that there was an attraction, and suddenly, she felt as guilty as if she had cheated on Jeff with another man when he was alive. She knew it was stupid to feel that way when absolutely nothing had happened, but she couldn't help it.

Robin remembered her mother telling her that Jeff would not want her to stay sad forever and would want her to find happiness with someone else, but she couldn't imagine that happening. She'd had other boyfriends, but she'd never been in love until she met Jeff. Their relationship made her understand that love was special, and it was different.

Robin imagined that someday she would go out with another man, but she wondered if she would ever fall in love again.

CHAPTER TWENTY-SIX

Elk Grove had its occasional domestic murder and fatal hit and run, but nothing worthy of front-page news on the criminal-law front had happened in a long time. Then Marjorie Loman came to town. Now its citizens were being entertained by headlines about kidnapped babies, and they flocked to the courthouse like cattle in a stampede, pushing and shoving to get a seat in the Honorable Mitchell Stonehouse's courtroom.

On Monday morning, the first day of the trial, Judge Stonehouse took up several defense motions, including the motion to bar the prosecution from introducing evidence about the murder of Joel Loman.

"What do you have to say, Mr. Hatcher?" the judge asked the prosecutor.

"Mrs. Loman has been calling herself Ruth Larson since she came to Elk Grove. That's what the Lindstroms knew her by. The jurors will learn that Ruth Larson is an alias, and they're going to want to know why she was lying about her name. We can't explain that without telling them that she's wanted for murder in Oregon and was hiding out here."

"Miss Lockwood?" Judge Stonehouse said.

"It's basic law that evidence has to be excluded if its prejudicial value outweighs its relevance. If you were teaching a law school class on evidence, Your Honor, you could use what Mr. Hatcher is trying to do as a perfect example of prosecutorial overreaching. How is Mrs. Loman going to get a fair trial if the jurors are told that the police in Oregon think she murdered her husband? An allegation, I assure you, Mrs. Loman vehemently denies."

The judge nodded. "I agree. We probably can't stop the witnesses from telling the jury that Mrs. Loman was calling herself Ruth Larson, but I'm not going to let you tell them that she's wanted on an unproven murder charge in Oregon."

"But, Your Honor . . . ," Hatcher started to argue.

Stonehouse held up his hand. "I've made my ruling on the Oregon murder charge."

Hatcher was upset that he wasn't going to be able to get in evidence of Joel Loman's murder, which he knew would prejudice the jury. But he also knew that he had to pick his battles, because Judge Stonehouse could make his life hell if he got on his wrong side.

"We'll take our morning recess and start jury selection when we reconvene," the judge said.

"Good job, Robin," Stan said when the judge left the courtroom.

"It's always nice to win a round. Let's hope it's not our only win."

After the Monday morning recess, the sides began jury selection, which they completed by the time court recessed on Tuesday afternoon. True to his word, Hatcher had asked the jurors if they'd heard about Robin's career in the Octagon and whether having a celebrity representing the defendant would influence their decision. A few jurors said they didn't know what Robin had done before practicing law, several potential jurors knew Robin had been on television but said that they would not be influenced by that fact, and a few people were dismissed when they admitted that Robin's status as a local hero might influence them.

On Wednesday morning, Robin followed Stan down the narrow aisle between the hard wooden benches on which the reporters and spectators sat and through a gate that was affixed to the low wooden barrier that separated nonparticipants from the area occupied by the judge, the bailiff, the court reporter, the attorneys, and their clients.

As she passed through the spectator section, Robin spotted her mother sitting with her sisters-in-law. Shirley had been opposed to Robin going to any law school instead of staying in Elk Grove, getting married, and bearing children, and Robin felt nervous about having to perform in front of her.

Moments after Robin took her seat at the defense table, the guards brought Marjorie into the courtroom. Stan had arranged to have Marjorie's hair styled in the jail. He'd also purchased several changes of clothing for her, and she looked neat and attractive in a dress Robin had helped Stan select.

"How are you holding up?" Stan asked.

"I didn't get much sleep last night."

"I'd be shocked if you had."

Marjorie had just taken her seat when the bailiff rapped the gavel and Judge Stonehouse entered the courtroom.

"Are the parties ready?" Judge Stonehouse asked when he took the bench.

As soon as both sides assured the court that they were, the judge nodded at the prosecuting attorney. "Your opening statement, Mr. Hatcher."

Hatcher rose slowly and walked to the jury box. "Good morning, ladies and gentlemen," he said as he made eye contact with the twelve members of the jury. "And thank you for doing your civic duty by serving on this sad and very serious case.

"Over the next few days, you will meet Emily and Caleb Lindstrom, a wonderful couple with a happy marriage who were missing something they wanted desperately, a child. Emily tried to get pregnant, but sadly, it was not to be, and the couple had almost given up on starting a family when Darrell Holloway, a local attorney, told them about surrogate mothers.

"A surrogate mother is a woman who agrees to carry a baby to term for a family when the wife is unable to become pregnant. In this instance, that woman was the defendant, whose real name is Marjorie Loman, but who came to Elk Grove using the alias Ruth Larson.

"You will learn that the defendant was paid fifty thousand dollars plus a monthly allowance and other benefits to have this baby. In order to earn this money, the defendant agreed, in writing, to give up all parental rights to the child. So, she knew from the get-go that the baby would be given to the Lindstroms the moment he was born and that she would cease to have any right to the child whatsoever.

"Ladies and gentlemen, the evidence will prove that soon after Roy Lindstrom was born, Marjorie Loman went to the Lindstroms' home and demanded baby Roy. When they refused to give her the baby and pointed out that she had signed away her parental rights, the defendant became abusive and threatened the Lindstroms.

"You will learn that the defendant became obsessed by her desire to have the baby. First, she hired a lawyer and sued them. Then, one evening, not satisfied to settle the matter in the courts, she took a gun to the Lindstroms' home, pistol-whipped Emily Lindstrom, and threatened to murder the couple if they didn't give her their child. The Lindstroms gave Marjorie Loman the child, and she ran away with him.

"That's when the defendant became a fugitive, wanted for the kidnapping of baby Roy and the assault on Emily Lindstrom that are charged in two of the counts in the indictment that has brought this matter to you.

"Several days after she kidnapped baby Roy, the defendant checked into a motel. The motel clerk recognized her and called 911. The police made sure that an ambulance and paramedics accompanied them to the motel, and it's very fortunate that they did. When the defendant was arrested and baby Roy was rescued, the paramedics saw that the baby had been seriously abused by the defendant."

Marjorie leaped to her feet. "That's a lie! I never hurt my baby."

Judge Stonehouse smashed his gavel down hard. "Control your client, Mr. McDermott."

"How can he say I would hurt Peter?" Marjorie shouted.

Robin placed an arm around Marjorie's shoulder.

"Please, Marjorie. Stan will tell the jury that you never hurt Peter."

Marjorie sagged against Robin. "I would never hurt my baby," she sobbed. "I love him."

"I know," Robin said as she eased Marjorie back onto her chair.

"If there's another outburst like that, Mrs. Loman, there will be serious consequences," the judge threatened. "Do you understand me?"

"She does, Your Honor," Stan assured the judge.

"I want to hear it from her," Judge Stonehouse insisted.

Robin whispered in Marjorie's ear and urged her to stand. Robin and Stan stood on either side of her.

"Did you understand me, Mrs. Loman? I will not put up with any more scenes."

Marjorie looked down and said, "I understand," in a voice that was barely above a whisper.

"Very well," the judge said. "You may continue, Mr. Hatcher."

"As I was saying, the police made sure that an ambulance staffed by paramedics Arlene Castro and Gary Pinsky was at the scene of the arrest. After baby Roy was rescued from the motel room, he was handed to Miss Castro. She will testify that baby Roy was in bad shape. There was swelling on the left side of his head, there were bruises on his lower back, and he had a seizure when they were taking him to the ambulance. Due to the paramedics' expert care, the baby stabilized by the time they arrived at the hospital emergency room.

"Nadine Wolfe is an emergency room doctor at King City General Hospital. Over the years, she has seen and treated many abused children. Some of these children don't have external injuries like a skull fracture or bruises on their upper bodies or arms, but they do have internal injuries that indicate that they have been abused.

"Until the 1970s, this was a mystery. How could a child suffer these serious internal injuries without evidence of external injuries? That's when a hypothesis was advanced that babies who exhibited subdural hemorrhages, retinal hemorrhages, and cerebral edema without evidence of external injuries must have been shaken very violently. Today, this explanation is widely accepted and is called shaken baby syndrome or abusive head trauma.

"Dr. Wolfe will tell you that it is her medical opinion that baby Roy was a victim of shaken baby syndrome and abusive head trauma, which was the result of the defendant subjecting baby Roy to violent shaking. That is the basis for the count in the indictment charging the defendant with assaulting baby Roy Lindstrom.

"Now, it is my duty as the person prosecuting this case to convince you that the defendant committed the crimes charged in the indictment. I am confident that when you've heard all the testimony in this case you will be convinced beyond a reasonable doubt that Marjorie Loman is guilty of assaulting Emily Lindstrom and kidnapping and assaulting the Lindstroms' baby. Thank you."

Hatcher sat down, and Stan walked over to the jury box.

"Good morning. Like Mr. Hatcher, I want to thank you for taking time to serve on Mrs. Loman's jury. Now, I'm sure you know from watching TV or civics classes in school that when the State accuses someone of wrongdoing in America, it has the complete burden of convincing you they're right. The flip side of that requirement is that Mrs. Loman has no obligation to present evidence, cross-examine witnesses, or do anything in this trial, because the accused in a criminal case is presumed to be innocent of wrongdoing. In other words, you have to start this trial with the assumption that the police got it wrong when they charged Mrs. Loman with these crimes.

"But putting the burden on the State to prove its case does present a problem that has to do with human nature. The State always puts on its evidence first, and it's natural to draw a conclusion about Mrs. Loman's guilt when you've only heard bad things being said about her. That's why I'm asking you not to draw any conclusions until you've heard our side.

"Let me give you an example. Mr. Hatcher told you that the presence of internal injuries like retinal hemorrhages and swelling brains in children without signs of external injury presented a mystery to the medical profession. He suggested that the mystery was solved in the 1970s using a theory called the shaken baby syndrome. Mrs. Loman is going to have you listen to Dr. Maxwell Lancaster, an eminent professor of pediatric pathology. He will tell you that the mystery has not been solved and that the State's explanation for Roy Lindstrom's injuries is way off base.

"I'm not going to take up any more time discussing the evidence in the case, because you will start hearing it as soon as I sit down. All I ask is that you keep an open mind and not jump to any conclusions until you've heard all the evidence, because I think you will have serious, reasonable doubts once all the evidence is in. Thank you."

Stan sat down, and the judge addressed the prosecutor.

"Mr. Hatcher, I understand Mr. Holloway is your first witness?"

"He is, Your Honor."

"Okay. Then let's get started."

As soon as Holloway was sworn, Hatcher established that he was an attorney practicing in Elk Grove. Then he asked Holloway to tell the jury what a surrogate did.

"Did Emily and Caleb Lindstrom tell you that doctors had determined that Emily was unable to conceive a child of her own?" Hatcher asked when the lawyer finished his explanation.

"Yes."

"Did they ask you to find a surrogate mother who would conceive their child?"

"Yes."

"Did you find a woman who was willing to become a surrogate?"

"Yes."

"Who was that woman?"

Holloway looked at Marjorie. "Mrs. Loman agreed to help the Lindstroms."

"Did the defendant agree to give up all parental rights to the baby the moment it was born?"

"Yes."

"How do you know this?"

"First, I explained it to her and entertained any questions she had. Then I had her read and sign a contract in which she agreed to relinquish her rights to the child."

"I'd like to enter State's Exhibit 4, Your Honor—a copy of the surrogacy contract that the defendant signed."

"No objection," Stan said.

"I have no more questions of the witness."

"Mr. McDermott?" the judge asked.

"Were there any problems with Mrs. Loman prior to giving birth?"

"None," Holloway said.

"What were the weather conditions when Mrs. Loman gave birth?"

"Elk Grove experienced one of the worst storms in her history," Holloway said.

"Did you or the Lindstroms make it to the hospital in time to see Mrs. Loman give birth?"

"No. We were never notified that Mrs. Loman was delivering the baby, and we may not have been able to get to the hospital even if we had been notified."

"Prior to Mrs. Loman going to the hospital to give birth, did you notify the hospital about Mrs. Loman's status as a surrogate?"

"Yes."

"Did you tell the hospital that, under no circumstances, was Mrs. Loman to have contact with the baby after he was born?"

"Yes."

"Were your instructions followed?"

"No."

"What happened?"

"There was a screwup, and a nurse gave Mrs. Loman the baby right after it was born. The baby stayed with her all night. I discovered the mistake in the morning when I brought the Lindstroms to the hospital."

"Did you notice a severe change in Mrs. Loman after she bonded with the baby?"

"Yes. She was hysterical and claimed that there was a conspiracy to keep the baby from her."

"Who was involved in this conspiracy?"

"I can't remember everyone, but it was the Lindstroms, the hospital. I think she thought that I was involved."

"Did you show her the contract she had signed in which she agreed to give up her parental rights?"

"I gave her a copy."

"What did she do with it?"

"She crumpled it up and threw it on the floor."

"No further questions."

Hatcher's next witness was Caleb Lindstrom. He testified that he and Emily had hired Darrell Holloway to procure a surrogate mother after a doctor told the Lindstroms that Emily could not conceive. Holloway had introduced the Lindstroms to the defendant, who agreed to carry their baby to term.

"Was there unusual weather on the evening that the defendant gave birth to Roy?" Hatcher asked.

"Yes, sir. There was a really bad snowstorm, one of the worst to ever hit Elk Grove."

"Did the storm prevent you from going to the hospital?"

"It might have if they'd called us to say that

Ruth . . ." Caleb turned toward Judge Stonehouse. "Can I call her Ruth Larson?"

"Well, Mr. Lindstrom, the defendant's real name is Marjorie Loman," the judge said. "So, you should refer to her as *Mrs. Loman* or *the defendant*."

"Okay. The hospital screwed up. From what I heard, they didn't know Mrs. . . . the defendant was a surrogate and we were supposed to get the baby right away, so they never called us."

"Did you come to the hospital the next morning?"

"Yes. Mr. Holloway found out about the problem and called us."

"And did you take Roy home?"

"Yes."

"How did being a new parent go?" Hatcher asked with a warm smile. Caleb had been very tense during his testimony, but he relaxed suddenly. "It was great," he answered enthusiastically. "Roy was real easy to love. He didn't fuss except to tell us he was hungry or needed his diaper changed, and he was very affectionate."

"So, life was good?"

Caleb stopped smiling. "Yeah, until she came around."

"To whom are you referring?" the prosecutor asked.

Caleb pointed at Marjorie. "The defendant."

"Please tell the jury about the first time the defendant came to your house after you took Roy home."

Caleb told the jury about Marjorie's demand that the Lindstroms give Roy to her and her hysterical outburst when they refused.

"What did you do after the defendant left?" Hatcher asked.

"Actually, she was still screaming and pounding on the door when I called Mr. Holloway to complain, but she left while I was talking to him."

"Was that the last time the defendant came to your house?"

"No, sir. The last time she came was when she stole our baby and hit my wife with a gun."

Hatcher picked up a revolver that had been lying on the prosecution table and walked over to Caleb Lindstrom. "Does this weapon look familiar?"

Caleb studied it for a moment before nodding. "The defendant hit Emily with that gun."

"Your Honor, the defense has agreed to stipulate that this weapon was seized from Mrs. Loman when she was arrested at the Prairie Lodge motel. I would like to introduce it into evidence."

"Any objection, Mr. McDermott?" the judge asked.

"No, Your Honor," Stan answered.

"It will be admitted. Anything more of this witness, Mr. Hatcher?"

"I have no further questions for Mr. Lindstrom."

"Mr. Lindstrom," Stan asked, "did the contract you, your wife, and Mrs. Loman entered into make it clear that Mrs. Loman was to have no contact with her baby as soon as she gave birth?"

"Yes."

"And that was to prevent her from bonding with her baby?"

"Yes."

"You testified that because of the chaos caused by the storm, the hospital made a terrible mistake and failed to notify you that Mrs. Loman had gone into labor."

"Yes."

"Did they compound the error by giving the baby to Mrs. Loman to feed and succor for hours after the birth?"

"Yes."

"Mrs. Loman's behavior during the two times she came to your house wasn't rational, was it?"

"Objection, Your Honor," Hatcher said as he sprang to his feet. "Mr. Lindstrom is not a psychiatrist."

"You don't have to be a psychiatrist to conclude that someone is acting crazy, Your Honor," Stan argued. "Mr. Lindstrom is perfectly capable of telling this jury what he saw and heard with his eyes and ears."

"I agree," the judge said. "Your objection is overruled, Mr. Hatcher. Mr. Lindstrom, you may answer the question."

"Was Mrs. Loman acting rationally on the two occasions she came to your house?"

"No. The first time she came to the house, she was screaming and calling Roy by a different name. The second time, she threatened to kill us, and she pistol-whipped my Emily."

"No further questions," Stan said.

Hatcher's next witness was Emily Lindstrom, who told the jury about being assaulted by Marjorie, the extent of her injuries, and the kidnapping.

"Mrs. Lindstrom," Stan asked when it was his turn to examine the witness, "how was Mrs. Loman acting on the evening she took your baby?"

"She was yelling and threatening. She said she'd kill us if we didn't give her Roy. Then she said she'd kill herself and Roy if we called the police."

"You named your baby Roy after your husband's father, didn't you?"

"Yes."

"Did Mrs. Loman call the baby Roy?"

"No, she used a different name."

"Does she call your baby Peter?"

"Yes, that's it."

"Roy is home now, isn't he?"

"Yes."

"Has he been examined by a doctor since he came home?"

"Yes."

"And he's doing fine?" asked Stan, who had interviewed the examining physician and read his reports.

"I . . . Yes."

"He's healthy and happy with no lasting trauma from the time Mrs. Loman was caring for him?"

"Objection, Your Honor," Hatcher said. "The defendant wasn't 'caring' for Roy. She kidnapped him."

"She did take Roy from the Lindstroms," Stan argued, "but it's the jury's job to determine if she abused him while he was with her."

"I'm going to sustain the objection to the use of the word *caring,* Mr. McDermott," the judge said.

Then he turned to the jurors. "No one is disputing that Mrs. Loman took the Lindstroms' baby or that the baby was with her for a period of time. The State has taken the position that Mrs. Loman abused the baby while he was with her. Mrs. Loman is arguing that she did not harm the baby while he was with her. Your job is to determine whether the State has proved, beyond a reasonable doubt, that the baby was abused, based on the evidence presented in this trial.

"You may continue examining the witness, Mr. McDermott."

"Does Roy appear to be a normal healthy baby now that he's back in your home?"

"Yes."

"No further questions."

Hatcher's next witness was Sam Forester, the King City chief of police who told the jury about the 911 call from the clerk that brought the police to the Prairie

Lodge motel and his call to Detective Guilford of the Elk Grove police force. Then he told the jurors about the arrest in Marjorie's motel room and how he took the baby to the paramedics.

"When you entered Mrs. Loman's motel room, where was the baby?" Stan asked when the prosecutor finished his direct examination.

"He was lying on a sleeping bag on the floor at the foot of the defendant's bed."

"How was he dressed?'

"He was in a diaper."

"Was he asleep?"

"He was, but the noise woke him up."

"Did he cry?"

"Yeah. There was a lot of noise and shouting, and I think that scared him."

"What did you do when you saw the baby?" Stan asked.

"My job during the arrest was to make sure he was safe. So, I picked him up really fast and ran to the ambulance."

"About what time in the morning did you raid the motel room?"

"I think it was sometime between two and three."

"I checked the weather report for that morning. If it said that the temperature was in the high thirties, does that sound right?"

"Yes."

"Nothing further."

Detective Guilford was next, and he told the jury about Marjorie Loman's arrest.

"Detective Guilford," Stan asked when he began his cross-examination, "Mrs. Loman was hysterical when you arrested her, wasn't she?"

"Yes."

"She was screaming and ranting?"

"Yes."

"What did she say?"

"She wasn't making a lot of sense. She was screaming for her baby, only she called him Peter, not Roy, and she said something about the doctors and the Lindstroms being out to get her."

"Can you be more specific?"

"Actually, no, I can't. She was putting up a lot of resistance, and I was concentrating on getting her under control. When we finally got her cuffed, she started crying, and she stopped talking except about wanting her baby."

"I've read your police report. In it, did you say that Mrs. Loman begged you not to hurt the baby?"

"Yes."

"So, she was concerned about the baby's safety?"

"That's what she said."

"No further questions."

"Who are your next witnesses, Mr. Hatcher?"

"Arlene Castro, one of the paramedics who took

charge of baby Roy and transported him to King City General Hospital. Then, I'm going to call Nadine Wolfe, the doctor who saw the baby in the emergency room."

"Okay. Well, I imagine they will take some time, so why don't we break for the day."

While the jurors were being escorted to the jury room, Robin looked at her client. Marjorie was weeping. Robin patted her shoulder.

"It all seems so hopeless," Marjorie said.

"Trust me. It's not," Robin assured her. "Stan did a good job laying a foundation for our case when he cross-examined the State's witnesses, and we have dynamite experts."

The guards led Marjorie out of the courtroom.

"She is so sad, it's killing me," Robin told Stan.

"Win or lose, Marjorie will always be sad about losing her baby," Stan said. "Our job is to get her out of this mess in one piece, so she can have a future that might include a kid of her own."

While Robin gathered her papers, she was surprised to see Roger Dillon leaving the courtroom.

"We may have a big problem," Robin told Stan.

"Oh?"

"Roger Dillon has been sitting in on our trial."

"Who is Roger Dillon?"

"He's one of the best homicide detectives in Portland."

"The case involving her husband?" Stan guessed.

"I can't think of any other reason he'd have for coming to Elk Grove."

"Don't tell Marjorie. She's got enough to worry about."

CHAPTER TWENTY-SEVEN

The next morning, Robin looked at the people waiting in the hall for court to start. She hoped Roger Dillon was one of them because she wanted to find out why he was in Elk Grove, but she didn't see him in the crowd.

When court began, a tall, muscular woman in the uniform of a paramedic took the stand. She had short black hair and serious brown eyes, and she carried herself like someone who was always ready to act in an emergency.

"Miss Castro, how are you employed?" Rodney Hatcher asked.

"I'm a paramedic."

"Can you tell the jury how you qualified to be a paramedic."

Castro turned to the jurors. "I graduated from high school before starting my training as an emergency medical technician, or EMT. The course included classroom work and about twelve hundred hours of practical training. I took community college courses in anatomy and physiology and was awarded an associate's degree. I had to develop various skills like dealing with fractures, bleeding, and cardiac and breathing emergencies. I learned how to administer intravenous fluids, some medications, and how to manage advanced equipment."

"Were you tested to see if you'd mastered these skills?"

"Yes, sir. After I finished my training, I took and passed written and practical exams given by the state."

"Okay. Let's move on to the evening when you went to the Prairie Lodge motel. Did you arrive at the motel in an ambulance?"

"Yes."

"After the defendant was arrested, did you take custody of a baby named Roy Lindstrom?"

"Yes."

"How did that happen?"

"Several police officers went into the defendant's motel room. Moments later, Sam Forester, the King City police chief, ran out with the baby and gave him to me and my partner, Gary Pinsky."

"Did anything about the baby's condition concern you?"

"There was a swelling on the left side of his head and some bruises on his lower back that were partially covered by his diaper."

"Did anything happen to baby Roy between the motel room and the ambulance?"

"Yes. The baby started shaking. I thought it might be a seizure or convulsions."

"What did you do to deal with the convulsions?"

"As soon as we got him in the ambulance, I laid him on a gurney, and we administered Ativan intravenously."

"Did that help?"

"Yes. Right after we left for the hospital, he stopped shaking."

"Did baby Roy have any trouble breathing?"

"Not at first. Our initial pulse oximetry reading was ninety-five percent. But it went down to eighty percent, he started turning blue, and his heart rate fell to fifty-five beats a minute."

"What did you do to deal with that problem?"

"I used an Ambu bag and mask to deliver one hundred percent oxygen while Gary administered CPR with chest compressions for a minute until the baby's heart rate came back to normal."

"Did you continue giving the baby oxygen until you arrived at the hospital?"

"Yes."

"Thank you, Miss Castro. I have no further questions."

"Mr. McDermott?" the judge said.

"Miss Lockwood will take this witness, Your Honor."

"Very well," Judge Stonehouse said.

"Miss Castro, was it still dark when the police arrested Mrs. Loman and brought you the baby?" Robin asked.

"Yes."

"What was the temperature?"

"I don't know exactly, but it was probably in the high thirties, low forties."

"Cold?"

"Yes."

"I believe you told the jurors that Roy was only wearing a diaper when he was taken from the motel room."

"Yes."

"Was he crying?"

"Yes."

"You told the jury that Roy began shaking while you were still in the parking lot, and the prosecutor characterized the shaking as convulsions."

"Yes."

"Is it possible that Roy, having been startled out of sleep, grabbed by a stranger, and rushed from a warm room into thirty-degree weather was simply shivering from the cold?"

"I guess that's one explanation."

"Miss Castro, when you took Roy from the police chief, was he breathing on his own?"

"Yes."

"You said that there were bruises on the baby's back."

"Yes."

"Was it dark in the parking lot?"

"Yes."

"How carefully did you examine the bruises?"

"I really didn't examine them at all. They were partially covered by the diaper. Then Roy was lying on his back from the time we put him on the gurney until we arrived at the hospital, so I couldn't see them."

"You mentioned swelling on the baby's head. Did you see a skull fracture, or was there anything that looked like a scalp laceration?"

"No."

"Are you aware that the medical records from the hospital in Elk Grove indicate that the swelling on the left side of the baby's head existed when the baby was born?"

"No."

"How long did it take you to get to the hospital?"

"Not long. Maybe fifteen, twenty minutes."

"Is it fair to say that the baby's oximeter reading and heart rate were normal when you arrived?"

"Yes."

"And he wasn't blue anymore? His color was normal?"

"Yes."

"No further questions, Your Honor."

"The State calls Dr. Nadine Wolfe, Your Honor."

A short woman with a runner's physique walked to the witness stand and took the oath. She was dressed in a conservative black dress, wore glasses with thick black rims, and her dark hair was gathered in a bun. Robin guessed that this was an attempt to make her look older, but she estimated that the witness was probably in her thirties and could have passed for a college student if she were wearing casual dress, her hair was down, and she ditched the glasses.

"Dr. Wolfe, where do you work?" Rodney Hatcher asked.

"I'm an emergency room doctor at King City General Hospital."

"Can you tell the jury about your education and training?"

"I grew up in South Dakota and went to college at Oberlin in Ohio. Then I was accepted at the medical school at the University of Chicago. That's a four-year program. The first two years, everyone studies anatomy, physiology, microbiology, the basic stuff you need to know to be a doctor. In my third year, I did a clinical rotation in emergency medicine, and I was hooked.

"Right after I was done with medical school, I started a three-year residency in emergency medicine at King City General Hospital."

"Did some of your training focus on treating babies who come to the emergency room at King City General Hospital?"

"Yes."

"How long have you been at King City?"

"I finished my residency two years ago. This is my second year as an attending physician."

"How many babies have you treated during your time at the hospital?"

"I'm not certain, but it's probably several hundred."

"Were you on duty in the emergency room when a baby named Roy Lindstrom was brought in?"

"Yes. I was the physician who examined him."

"Were you briefed by Arlene Castro and Gary Pinsky, the paramedics who transported Roy to the hospital?"

"Yes."

"What did they tell you?"

"They said that Roy had been rescued from a kidnapper at the Prairie Lodge motel and had been handed off to them at the scene by a police officer. They said that Roy had some odd shaking movements at the scene that might have been convulsions, but they had given him Ativan intravenously and the shaking had stopped. They also pointed out swelling on the left side of the baby's head and bruises on the baby's back.

"On the way to the hospital, the baby's heart rate had slowed to fifty-five beats per minute, and he had looked blue, but they had given him oxygen and administered CPR until the heart rate came back up. They reported that the oximeter reading, cyanosis, and heart rate were all normal by the time they arrived at King City General."

"Did your initial observations of baby Roy mesh with the conclusions of the paramedics?"

"Yes. Roy was breathing on his own, and his respiratory rate, heart rate, blood pressure, and pulse oximeter readings were all normal."

"You mentioned that the EMTs made you aware that Roy had been rescued from a kidnapper?"

"Yes."

"Did that raise the possibility that the baby had been abused?"

"That and the swelling on his head and the bruises."

"Did you examine Roy to see if there were signs that he had been abused?"

"Yes."

"Please tell the jurors about your examination."

"Okay. Well, I noticed extensive bruising on the baby's lower back and buttocks. A large swelling on the left side of the head made me concerned about the possibility of an old or new skull fracture, and the convulsions the EMTs told me about suggested possible brain damage. Roy's head appeared large. I measured it, and the head circumference was at the ninety-seventh percentile for his age. As a result of the observations that I made of Roy's head, I decided to perform a CT scan."

"What is a CT scan?" Hatcher asked.

"A CT scan, or computed tomography scan, is a medical imaging procedure that uses computer-processed combinations of many x-ray measurements taken from different angles to produce cross-sectional images of specific areas of a scanned object. This let me see inside Roy's skull without having to cut into it."

"What did the CT scan show?"

"The radiologist report indicated that there were subdural fluid collections over the frontal lobes. That usually means bleeding has occurred in the area just in front of the brain. The report said that the lateral ventricles were normal size. There was no cerebral edema, but the radiologist said there was a bony swelling of the skull on the left side."

"Was there any evidence of a fracture?" the prosecutor asked.

"No."

"Go on."

"I examined Roy's eyes and thought I saw retinal

hemorrhages. It's hard to examine the eyes of a squirming baby, but I thought there was bleeding in the retinas."

"Did you consult a pediatric ophthalmologist after seeing the retinal hemorrhages?"

"Yes. I called in Dr. Gwen Harper."

"What did she tell you?"

"She confirmed the presence of the hemorrhages."

"Now, you told the jury that you did not find a skull fracture."

"That's correct."

"Did you find any other external signs of abuse?"

"There were the bruises, but they appeared to be old. I did not see any marks on the baby's arms or chest that would indicate an impact."

"What conclusion did you come to after you completed your examination of baby Roy?"

"I concluded that his injuries were the result of abuse and not accidental."

"How did you come to this conclusion?"

"When doctors consider child abuse, we often think about the shaken baby syndrome. More recently, the term used is *abusive head trauma* because there may actually be blunt trauma or an impact in addition to the shaking."

"Can you tell the jury how you arrive at this diagnosis?"

"Sure. The diagnosis of shaken baby syndrome

emerged in the 1970s when some physicians began advancing the hypothesis that if an infant or young child became very ill or died without an obvious reason, and the baby exhibited three things, usually referred to as the *triad* of findings, then the cause of his injuries might be violent shaking."

"What is the 'triad'?"

"First, we find blood in the subdural area around the brain, a subdural hemorrhage. Second, there is microscopic bleeding in the retina, or retinal hemorrhages. Finally, there is encephalopathy, which may show up as vomiting, irritability, feeding problems, convulsions, apnea, or brain swelling, called *cerebral edema*."

"When this violent shaking occurs, what is going on inside the baby?" Hatcher asked.

"What we believe happens is that through anger or frustration, an adult will pick up a baby, usually by the chest, arms, or other part of the body, and shake the baby back and forth or side to side violently enough so the chin hits the chest, the back of the head hits the back, or the ears hit the side. Babies have weak necks, so shaking their bodies can cause their heads to really whip around a lot.

"In the process of shaking back and forth, the brain bangs forcefully against the inside of the bony, hard skull. This trauma causes bruising and bleeding in the brain.

"At the same time that's happening, the blood vessels that cross from the brain through the coverings of the brain, or dura, can rupture and start to bleed. The blood that collects between tho brain and the dura is called a *subdural hematoma.*

"The second component of the triad is the retinal hemorrhages. The shaking can cause the blood vessels in the back of the eye, called the *retina,* to tear and bleed. Another theory is that the retinal bleeding comes from increased blood pressure or increased intracranial or intrathoracic pressure.

"The third part of the triad is encephalopathy. Because the nerves and the brain cells are damaged, chemicals are released that cause an intense inflammatory reaction. Enzymes are released that cause small blood vessels to leak fluid, which causes the brain to swell up, just like your ankle swells up when you injure it.

"We also know that shaking back and forth and side to side is like a concussion, which can cause the part of the brain that makes us breathe to stop functioning. So, a baby that's severely shaken may stop breathing, which decreases the flow of blood, which deprives the brain of oxygen, which can cause more damage to the baby's brain cells."

"Did you reach a conclusion to a reasonable medical certainty about whether Roy's injuries were caused by abuse as opposed to being accidental?"

"Yes."

"What was your conclusion?"

"Based on the head swelling, the bruising on the back, the subdural hematomas, the retinal hemorrhages, and the convulsions, I believe Roy Lindstrom's injuries were the result of child abuse."

"I have no further questions of Dr. Wolfe, Your Honor," Hatcher said.

Stan had investigated Dr. Wolfe's background, and Robin reviewed his notes before addressing the witness.

"Good afternoon, Dr. Wolfe," Robin said. "Am I correct that your specialty is emergency medicine?"

"Yes."

"Are you board certified in pediatric pathology?"

"No."

"How about forensic pathology?"

"No."

"Isn't it true that you really don't have any specialized training in pediatrics, other than some monthlong rotations at the children's hospital?"

"Yes, but I do treat children who come into the emergency room."

"Am I correct in stating that when you treat a child in the emergency room, it's in your role as an emergency room doctor and not as a pediatrician?"

"Yes."

"During your direct examination, you stated that

you had been told that Roy had been rescued from a kidnapper."

"Yes."

"Did that make you predisposed to assume the baby had been abused?"

"No. I would have conducted my examination in the same way."

"You are aware, are you not, that there are a broad range of nontraumatic or accidental causes that can account for the triad of subdural hemorrhages, retinal hemorrhages, and swelling of the brain in infants, including accidental trauma, short falls, prenatal conditions, congenital malformations, disease, metabolic disorders, hypoxia, childhood stroke, infection, brain injury, rebleeds, and toxins?"

"Yes."

"Would you have considered these explanations if the paramedics had told you that they were bringing you Roy because a nice, middle-class mother had called 911?"

Dr. Wolfe stiffened. "I treat all children the same."

"You testified that the theory that the triad is caused by shaking a baby violently was created in the 1970s by a hypothesis that sought to explain how these internal injuries could occur without any external signs of injury like a skull fracture or bruises."

"Yes."

"In science, when you develop a hypothesis, don't

you usually conduct experiments to see if you can prove you're on the right track?"

"Yes."

"Isn't it also true that there has never been a single experiment that involved shaking a human baby that has been conducted to see if you can create the triad simply by shaking a baby violently?"

Dr. Wolfe laughed. "An experiment like that with real babies would be totally unethical."

"So, your answer is that no one has ever shown that shaken baby syndrome is an accurate explanation for the triad absent external injuries with an experiment using babies?"

"I . . . Yes."

"Can this jury conclude that doctors who accept the syndrome have done so without the rigorous experimentation to which all other scientific theories are subjected?"

"You can't test it by shaking babies. That would be criminal."

"Are you aware of experiments that were devised to test the theory using biomechanics?"

"Yes."

"Isn't it true that a neurosurgeon named Tina Duhaime tried to duplicate the force claimed to cause the triad in test dummies in the late 1980s and couldn't?"

"I've heard about her experiments."

"Are you aware that using the same dummies that

are used in crash tests by the automotive industry and NASA, football players who shook these dummies thousands of times could not generate enough force to cause the injuries you see in the triad?"

"There's a difference between using an inanimate object and shaking a human baby."

"Will you concede that there has never been an experimental model using biomechanics that confirms that you can shake a baby hard enough to create injuries inside the head like the injuries you've called the triad?"

"I don't know enough about those studies to offer an opinion."

"Will you concede that the diagnosis of shaken baby syndrome or abusive head trauma is no longer universally accepted?"

"It is widely accepted in the medical profession, but there is a small, vocal minority that have questioned its validity."

"Have you heard of the Goudge Inquiry, a commission that was formed in 2008 in Ontario, Canada?"

"I think so."

"Isn't it true that the commission concluded that there had been twenty-plus false convictions for child abuse homicide on the basis of the shaken baby syndrome?"

"I haven't read the report."

"Then you're not aware that after listening to experts

from all over the world, the commission concluded that a diagnosis of abuse should not be based on the mere existence of the triad?"

"I don't know what they concluded. But I would disagree with that conclusion."

"Do you also disagree with a similar conclusion that was reached in England when more individuals were released from prison for false convictions based on the syndrome?"

"I haven't read about that."

"Are you aware of a 2008 Wisconsin case, where the Wisconsin Court of Appeals reviewed a shaken baby case and wrote that there is fierce disagreement among doctors about the shaken baby diagnosis that is signaling a shift in mainstream medical opinion?"

"I have not read that case."

"Let's talk about the retinal hemorrhages. You called in a pediatric ophthalmologist to examine Roy's eyes, didn't you?"

"Yes."

"And didn't Dr. Harper tell you that the retinal hemorrhages were few in number and superficial?"

"Yes."

"That would be consistent with a non-abuse cause, wouldn't it?"

"It could be either."

"So, you can't say beyond a reasonable doubt that abuse caused the retinal hemorrhages, can you?"

"No."

"One last question. Were you aware that the record of Roy Lindstrom's birth indicates that the swelling you saw at King City General Hospital existed when the Lindstroms' baby was born?"

"I . . . No, I didn't know that."

"Thank you, Dr. Wolfe. I have no further questions."

After conducting a short redirect examination of Dr. Wolfe, Rodney Hatcher rested the State's case and the judge dismissed the jury.

"I assume you have some motions to make, Mr. McDermott," Judge Stonehouse said when the jurors were gone.

"We do."

"Let's take them up in the morning."

The judge recessed court and left the bench.

"Want to grab a bite to eat and do a postmortem?" Stan asked after the guards left with Marjorie.

"Sounds good. Let's do Buster's. I'm beat, and I need some red meat."

"How do you think we're doing?" Robin asked when they were outside the courthouse and away from anyone who might be interested in Stan's answer.

"I'm feeling pretty good after your cross of the paramedic and Dr. Wolfe. I think you scored some points, especially with the questions about the retinal hemorrhages and the fact that there was swelling when the baby was born. I was watching the jurors when you attacked the shaken baby diagnosis, and I think you've got some of them thinking. More important, you've laid the groundwork for our experts. What do you think?"

"I didn't think that Dr. Wolfe was super impressive. Dr. Lancaster's credentials are way better, and he should make mincemeat out of the abuse allegations. It's the kidnapping charge that worries me."

"You've put together a good defense, Robin."

"On paper. I'm not sure it will fly in the real world."

"That brings up a question of trial strategy. Do we call Marjorie as a witness?"

"I don't think we can risk it. We aren't contesting the fact that she kidnapped the baby and assaulted Emily Lindstrom. What we have is a technical defense. We're arguing that the medical diagnosis Dr. Wolfe made is wrong. Nothing Marjorie could say would help there."

"She can deny shaking Roy."

"The jurors might not believe her. She'd have every reason to lie. And Dr. Lancaster will blow the diagnosis of shaken baby out of the water."

"Which brings us to the kidnapping," Stan said.

Robin smiled. "We're going to argue that Marjorie is nuts, and in a way, she already testified in her own behalf when she went crazy in court."

"So, you think we shouldn't call her?"

"If we have any chance of getting an acquittal on the kidnapping and assault charges, it will come from Dr. Suarez's testimony."

Robin could hear the television going in the living room when she opened the door to her house.

"Hi, Mom. What are you watching?"

Shirley paused the show. "It's a *Perry Mason* rerun I recorded."

Robin laughed. "I didn't know you watched *Perry Mason*."

Shirley blushed. "I started watching when you started working for that Barrister woman. I wanted to see what you thought was so interesting about representing criminals."

Robin loved *Perry Mason*. After the lawyer her father had hired forced the school board to let her wrestle on the boys' team, Robin decided that she was going to be a lawyer. Once she'd decided on her career, she devoured every one of Erle Stanley Gardner's Perry Mason novels and became a devoted fan of the television show. Sometimes, when she was having trouble figuring out how to approach a case, Robin would ask herself what Perry would do.

Robin sat down next to her mother. "Do you figure out whodunit before Perry reveals the murderer?"

"Sometimes. But I'm usually fooled."

"You know that criminals don't jump up and confess in real life, don't you?"

Shirley scowled. "Of course, and I also know that most of the people our police arrest aren't innocent like they are in the TV shows."

"What about Marjorie Loman? You've been in court every day. Do you think she's innocent?"

Shirley didn't answer right away, and Robin could see that she was taking the question seriously.

"I didn't at first about hurting the baby after Mr. Hatcher gave his argument to the jury. But I'm not so sure now after hearing what you said about that syndrome."

"What about the other charges?"

"Oh, she's guilty of kidnapping the baby and hitting poor Mrs. Lindstrom. I don't have any doubts about that."

"What about Dana and the other wives? What do they think?"

"Well, we talked about it over lunch. Claire thinks she's guilty of hurting the baby, but Dana and Rosemarie aren't so sure. Everyone agrees that she should go to jail for hitting Mrs. Lindstrom with the pistol and kidnapping baby Roy."

"Hopefully, you'll change your mind when you've heard our witnesses."

"I'm keeping an open mind."

"Good," Robin said as she stood up. "I'm going to do some prep for tomorrow. Then I'm going to sleep. Go on back to your show."

Robin kissed her mother on the cheek and went upstairs. She was pleased that Shirley and two of the wives had questions about the child abuse charge, but it was clear that getting an acquittal on the kidnapping and assault was going to be an uphill battle.

CHAPTER TWENTY-EIGHT

When court started in the morning, Robin moved for a judgment of acquittal on the child abuse charge, arguing that the shaken baby syndrome was not an adequate basis for proving that Marjorie had caused injuries to Roy Lindstrom, absent external evidence of abuse. As expected, Judge Stonehouse denied the motion. As soon as the jury was seated, the judge told the defense to call its first witness.

"Mrs. Loman calls Dr. Maxwell Lancaster as her witness," Robin told the court, and a man straight out of central casting walked to the stand.

Dr. Lancaster's height was not quite six feet, but his perfect posture made him appear taller. He had snow-white hair and a neatly trimmed snow-white beard. If he'd been portly, the twinkle in his eye and his gentle smile would have brought Santa to mind, but his compact, muscular build made most people conclude that he'd once been an athlete who had maintained his fitness, which would have been on the mark.

"Dr. Lancaster, how are you employed?" Robin asked.

"I'm a professor of pediatric pathology at the medical school at the Oregon Health Sciences University in Portland, Oregon."

"What does a pediatric pathologist do?"

"On television, pathologists perform autopsies, but we do a lot more. We use laboratory tests to study the causes of disease. In fact, the pathology department oversees all aspects of running the clinical labs that do things like blood and urine tests and bacterial cultures. We also examine biopsy specimens that surgeons send us to see whether there are signs of cancer or other diseases."

"When you say that you are a professor, does that mean that you only teach in a classroom?"

"No. I teach medical students, interns, residents, and other doctors in various settings. I do give lectures in a classroom, but most of my teaching is done either in the lab or the autopsy room."

"Can you tell the jury where you went to college?"

"I did my undergraduate degree in physics, with a minor in biology, at the University of California at Berkeley."

"Did you have an academic scholarship?"

Lancaster smiled. "No, it was an athletic scholarship. I was on the college tennis team."

"How did you do?"

"I was an All-American my junior and senior year."

"Did you play professionally after you graduated?"

"Yes, for two years. Then I blew out my knee and decided to go to medical school."

"What medical school did you attend?"

"Harvard. Then I did my four-year residency in anatomic and clinical pathology at the University of Pennsylvania, followed by a one-year pediatric pathology fellowship at the Children's Hospital of Philadelphia. Following that, I did a one-year fellowship in forensic pathology at the University of New Mexico."

"Are you board certified in pathology?"

"Yes. I took all the exams, and I am board certified in pathology, pediatric pathology, and forensic pathology."

"Did I ask you to review the medical records of a child named Roy Lindstrom?"

"Yes."

"What records did you review?"

"Everything from his records from the hospital where he was born, his pediatrician's records, his charts from King City General Hospital. I got skull x-rays, CT scans, a workup by a pediatric ophthalmologist."

"Did I also give you police reports and the transcript of the testimony of Dr. Nadine Wolfe and a paramedic named Arlene Castro?"

"Yes."

"Are you aware of Dr. Wolfe's diagnosis that Roy was injured as a result of child abuse and violent shaking?"

"Yes."

"Do you agree with her?"

"Absolutely not."

"Can you please tell the jury why you disagree?"

Dr. Lancaster turned toward the jurors. "I disagree for two reasons. First, I don't believe that the shaken baby syndrome, or abusive head trauma, is a valid basis for making an evaluation that abuse has occurred. Second, and more important, I disagree with Dr. Wolfe's opinion that the Lindstrom child suffered injuries, much less injuries caused by abuse."

"Okay, then. Let's tackle the syndrome first. Why don't you believe it is a valid basis for giving an opinion that abuse caused problems that a baby may be experiencing?"

"You made several points during your cross-examination of Dr. Wolfe that bear repeating. Many years ago, child abuse experts felt that when there were no external signs of abuse, the triad of subdural hematomas, retinal hemorrhages, and encephalopathy or cerebral edema had to be caused by violent shaking because nothing else explained those injuries absent external signs of abuse.

"You have to understand that child abuse, like spousal abuse, was largely under-recognized and frequently ignored during most of the twentieth century. So, concerned physicians began campaigns to educate other doctors and parents about the problem. Even though data about the effect of jolting, whiplash, and jerking of infants was incomplete and circumstantial, a national educational campaign was launched. At the time, these physicians never envisioned or advocated using their findings in criminal prosecutions, but that's what happened, even though no experiments ever showed that shaking a baby produced the triad."

"Dr. Wolfe pointed out that it would be totally unethical and probably criminal to experiment with babies," Robin said.

"And that's the problem. In medical science, we get an idea about the cause of a disease or injury that may be right but may be wrong. Before you start telling people that you have an explanation for the cause of the disease or injury, you do experiments. But you can't do that in the case of shaken baby, so it's wrong to prosecute people based on an unproven theory."

"Was that the conclusion of the Goudge Inquiry in Canada, another commission in England, and the Wisconsin Court of Appeals that I discussed with Dr. Wolfe?"

"Yes. Equally important are the biomechanical experiments that failed to produce the degree of force necessary to cause the triad. So, we don't have any experimental evidence to support the syndrome or abusive head trauma theories."

"Let's move on to the facts in Mrs. Loman's case. Mrs. Loman and the baby were in a warm room in a motel when the room was raided. Roy was on the floor sleeping on a sleeping bag dressed in a diaper and nothing else when the police broke into the room. According to the State's witnesses, the baby was startled out of sleep, scooped up by a police officer he didn't know, and carried outside into thirty-degree weather. At which point he began to shake. The paramedics thought that Roy was having a seizure and gave him intravenous Ativan to stop the shaking. Do you have a medical opinion about this situation? If so, what is it?"

"I can tell you that Roy has not had any record of seizures or convulsions up to the day he was taken to King City General, and an EEG—a brain wave test—did not demonstrate any seizures or epilepsy. So, I think he probably didn't have a seizure in the parking lot."

"How do you explain the shaking?" Robin asked.

"He might just have been cold after being frightened by the noise generated by the raid, grabbed by someone he didn't know, and brought very abruptly from a warm room into thirty-degree weather clad only in a diaper.

"He may also have been demonstrating neonatal shudders or tremors. These are seen in healthy newborns and are largely benign. But they can be concerning to parents who confuse them with seizures."

"What about the bruises on Roy's back and buttocks?" Robin asked.

Dr. Lancaster smiled. "I looked at the photos. They're not bruises. Roy has hyperpigmented areas called *Mongolian spots*. They are a type of birthmark you usually see on the lower back, buttocks, and legs. It's more common in African American babies, but you see it in about ten percent of Caucasian babies. They're not dangerous, there isn't any treatment for them, and they usually disappear by age six. I can see how someone like Dr. Wolfe, who hasn't had specialized training in pediatrics, might confuse Mongolian spots with bruising."

"What about the slow breathing and respiration problems that Roy experienced on the way to the hospital? Do you think that's from brain damage?"

"The most logical explanation for what happened on the ride to the hospital is that Roy's respirations slowed down and he required mask breathing because the paramedics gave him Ativan for what they mistakenly thought was a seizure. Ativan can cause respiratory depression in babies. If he'd had breathing problems from brain damage, the problems would not have been resolved so quickly."

"Dr. Wolfe told this jury that one reason she thought Roy was abused was because he had swelling on the left side of his head. Do you have an opinion about that?"

"I do."

"What is it?"

"I've studied the x-rays that were taken of Roy's skull. They do not show a fracture. I also reviewed the records of Roy's birth. It was prolonged and forceps were used during the delivery, and the records note that there was swelling on the left side of the baby's head when he was born. It is my opinion that the swelling is actually a remnant of a cephalohematoma, which is a hemorrhage of blood between the skull bone and the periosteum, which is common in prolonged labor or forceps deliveries. They usually resolve within weeks or months of birth. In the healing process, the blood forms a clot and calcifies, creating a bony, hard swelling in the head. In general, they don't require treatment."

"What about the retinal hemorrhages that Dr. Harper noticed?"

"Retinal hemorrhages caused by severe head trauma are usually large and numerous, involve multiple layers of the retina, and may involve splitting or tearing of the retina. Roy's retinal hemorrhages are few in number and superficial. Many experts think retinal hemorrhage can be caused by increased intrathoracic pressure caused by chest compressions, so there's a good chance that they were caused by the CPR compressions administered by the EMTs."

"What about the subdural collection mentioned by the radiologist in the CT scan report?"

"Several things, other than abusive head trauma, can cause subdural fluid collections. Birth-related bleeding can do it and may take a few months to resolve. In some kids, non-bloody fluid can slowly leak into the subdural space for several months. We call that a *chronic subdural effusion,* or *hygroma*. The increased fluid spreads the skull bones apart and results in a large head. Remember, Roy's head circumference was very large, so I think chronic effusion is a likely explanation for what the radiologist saw on the CT scan."

"Is there anything else that causes you to question Dr. Wolfe's conclusion that Roy suffered abuse?"

"I saw a skeletal survey of Roy, which didn't show any old or new fractures, and all his laboratory tests, including tests for blood clotting, were normal."

"So, to wrap up, Dr. Lancaster, do you have an opinion to a reasonable medical certainty about whether Roy is a victim of child abuse?"

"I do."

"What is that opinion?"

"I don't believe there is any evidence of abuse. All the findings can be explained by mechanisms other than shaking or child abuse. I believe that Roy Lindstrom was a perfectly healthy child when he was taken from the motel room at the Prairie Lodge motel."

"No further questions, Your Honor."

"Mr. Hatcher?"

"Thank you, Your Honor," Hatcher said as he turned toward the witness. "Dr. Lancaster, you weren't in King City General Hospital on the night that baby Roy was brought in, were you?"

"No."

"And unlike Dr. Wolfe, you did not examine the baby personally?"

"No."

"Now, you have suggested that the shaken baby syndrome is not a proven hypothesis and should not be used to diagnose child abuse. Would you concede that your view is a minority view?"

"It is a view that is gaining wider acceptance all the time."

"But it is not the view of a majority of pediatricians, is it?"

"No."

"You told the jury several alternative explanations for Roy's injuries."

"Yes."

"But isn't it true that that is all they are, alternatives?

Isn't it possible that Dr. Wolfe, who had firsthand contact with Roy, got it right?"

"I don't believe so. She misdiagnosed the Mongolian spots and overestimated the importance of the retinal hemorrhages, which are too few in number to support a finding of abuse, among other things. She also did not know that the swelling of Roy's head had occurred when he was delivered. Dr. Wolfe may be a competent emergency room physician, but she does not have expertise in pediatric pathology, which provides the training she would need to make a competent diagnosis of abuse in this case."

Hatcher realized that he was not going to make any headway with Dr. Lancaster. If he asked any more questions, he would give the witness more opportunities to repeat his opinion that Roy had not been abused.

"Nothing more, Your Honor," Hatcher said.

"Miss Lockwood?"

"We'd ask that the witness be excused."

"Very well," Judge Stonehouse said. "It's getting late, so we'll recess and resume Monday morning."

CHAPTER TWENTY-NINE

Stan and Robin thanked Dr. Lancaster for his testimony, then Stan had Ray Flores, one of his associates, drive Dr. Lancaster to the airport. The attorneys did a postmortem as they walked back to the office. Robin was feeling upbeat about the impact of the doctor's testimony, and she felt that it was a great advantage to have Dr. Lancaster as the last witness before court recessed for the weekend, because the jurors would have two days to think about his very favorable testimony. But the feeling soon wore off. Dr. Lancaster had dealt a blow to Hatcher's chances of getting a guilty verdict on the child abuse charge, but the kidnapping and assault charges were still in play, and they had always been the charges that worried her the most.

Robin spent most of Saturday at Stan's law office

working on jury instructions and legal motions. Dinner with the family on Saturday evening took her mind off the case, but she plunged back in when Dr. Gabrielle Suarez arrived in Elk Grove. The psychiatrist was Marjorie's only hope of winning an acquittal on the kidnapping and assault charges, and Robin spent several hours on Sunday afternoon going over her testimony. Then Stan and the two women went to dinner, where they talked about everything but the case.

Monday morning, Stan and Robin escorted Dr. Suarez to the courthouse. Before escorting her into the courtroom, Robin told her that she would be their second witness.

Moments after the judge took the bench, Robin called Nancy Cleary to the stand. Cleary was a sturdily built woman in her early thirties with a round face, auburn hair, green eyes, and milk-white skin. She looked nervous when she took the oath, and she looked unsure of herself when she took her place in the witness-box.

"What do you do for a living?" Robin asked.

"I'm a nurse."

"Do you work at the hospital in Elk Grove?"

"Yes."

"Were you on duty when Marjorie Loman gave birth?"

"Yes."

"Where had you been the day before?"

"My husband and I flew back from a vacation in Hawaii."

Robin smiled at the witness to put her at ease. "Was there much difference in the weather in Hawaii and Elk Grove?"

That got a smile out of Cleary. "I'll say. It was sunny and warm when we left Oahu, and we landed at the start of one of the worst winter storms in Elk Grove history."

"But you made it to work in the morning?"

"Just."

"Was Mrs. Loman in labor when she arrived at the hospital?"

"Yes."

"Was the delivery very difficult?"

"It was long, and she was in a lot of pain."

"Did the doctor have to use forceps to help with the birth?" Robin asked.

"Yes."

"Were you still jet-lagged when you arrived for work?"

"I was."

"Do you think that had something to do with the mistake you made after Mrs. Loman gave birth?" Robin asked as she threw the nurse a lifeline.

"It probably contributed to it," Cleary answered, grateful that Robin was going easy on her.

"Please tell the jury what went wrong after Roy was born."

"There were notes in Mrs. Loman's chart that told the staff that she was a surrogate mother who was carrying her baby to term for Emily and Caleb Lindstrom. The notes said that the baby was to be given to the Lindstroms as soon as he was born and that Mrs. Loman was to have no contact with the baby. In all the confusion with the storm and the problems with the delivery, I never read the notes, and I made the mistake of giving Roy to Mrs. Loman after the birth."

"Were the Lindstroms at the hospital?" Robin asked.

"No. They would have had trouble getting there because of the weather, but I've heard that they weren't notified that Mrs. Loman was in labor."

"Did Mrs. Loman spend the night feeding Roy and bonding with him?" Robin asked.

"Yes."

"Did you sleep at the hospital that night?"

"Yes, because of the storm. I didn't want my husband driving to pick me up. It was too dangerous."

"Was the mistake put right in the morning?"

"Yes. Mr. Holloway, the Lindstroms' lawyer, told them to come to the hospital, and he came too. That's when I learned that Mrs. Loman was a surrogate mother. Mr. Holloway was very upset when he learned that the baby was with Mrs. Loman. As soon as I learned about the surrogacy, I went to Mrs. Loman's room and took the child to the Lindstroms."

"Was Mrs. Loman asleep when you took the baby from her room?"

"Yes."

"What happened when she woke up and learned that Roy was gone forever?"

"She became hysterical."

"Did you give a statement to the police in which you described Mrs. Loman's actions upon learning that her baby had been taken from her?"

"Yes," Cleary said, choking up as she answered.

"How did you describe her reaction?"

"She . . ." Cleary licked her lips. "I said that she howled like an animal whose cub had been torn from her."

"No further questions, Your Honor," Robin said.

When she returned to her seat, Robin noticed that several of the women on the jury and two of the men looked upset.

"Mr. Hatcher?"

"No questions, Your Honor."

"Call your next witness."

"Mrs. Loman calls Dr. Gabrielle Suarez," Robin said.

Dr. Suarez was a slender woman in her midforties with jet-black hair and dark-complexioned skin. The psychiatrist was dressed in a conservative navy-blue suit and white silk blouse, and she wore a graceful string of pearls around her neck.

"Dr. Suarez, how are you employed?" Robin asked.

"I'm a professor of psychiatry at the Stanford University School of Medicine in Palo Alto, California."

"Can you tell the jury about your educational and professional background?"

"I grew up in New York City and graduated from New York University with a degree in psychology. I spent two years in the Peace Corps in the Dominican Republic. As part of my duties, I translated for teams of doctors who ran clinics in remote areas, did plastic surgery for burn victims and children with cleft palates, and performed other surgeries and other medical procedures. That was my inspiration to go to medical school."

"Where did you go?"

"I received an M.D. from Duke University School of Medicine in Durham, North Carolina, and decided to become a psychiatrist. I did my residency at the University of Washington School of Medicine in Seattle."

"Is there an area of psychiatry in which you have specialized?"

"Yes. Over the years, I have become interested in psychiatric problems that develop in mothers."

"Have you written and lectured on these issues?"

"Yes, extensively."

"Your Honor, I'd like to have Dr. Suarez's curriculum vitae, which lists her education, her publications, and the lectures she has given, admitted as Defense Exhibit 17."

"Mr. Hatcher?" the judge asked.

"No objection."

"Are you aware that Marjorie Loman acted as a surrogate for Caleb and Emily Lindstrom?"

"Yes."

"Have you read police reports of interviews with witnesses and the testimony of witnesses that have detailed the birth of Mrs. Loman's baby, now named Roy Lindstrom, and her interactions with the Lindstroms?"

"I have."

"Have you read medical reports detailing her delivery of baby Roy?"

"Yes."

"And have you spent time talking with Mrs. Loman?"

"Yes. We've met on three occasions."

"What have you learned about Mrs. Loman's behavior during and following the birth of her baby that you believe the jurors need to know?"

Dr. Suarez turned toward the jury box. "Mrs. Loman went through a very hard delivery. It was prolonged and involved the use of a forceps to deliver the baby. In some women, this type of delivery can trigger a bipolar episode that can lead to a condition known as *postpartum psychosis.*"

"What is a psychosis?"

"Psychosis is a condition that affects the way your brain processes information. It causes an individual to lose touch with reality. People in the grip of psychosis might see, hear, or believe things that aren't real. Extreme stress or trauma can cause it."

"What is postpartum psychosis?"

"Postpartum psychosis is a severe mental health condition that can arise suddenly in new mothers. It is a lapse of sanity that can cause a new mother to lose touch with reality. As a pregnancy moves along, hormones shift gradually. But during a delivery, estrogen and progesterone plummet. As the mother's body struggles to adapt to post-pregnancy, postpartum psychosis distorts the new mother's perception of reality. She can experience insomnia, paranoia, delusions, and even auditory and visual hallucinations."

"Are there reasons why a surrogate mother might develop this psychosis?"

"When a surrogate gives birth, her experience is quite different from a mother who gives birth to a child of her own and takes the baby home. For the surrogate, there is a sudden shift in her daily routine that can cause feelings of loss. Prior to giving birth, she is in constant communication with doctors and the intended parents, but once the parents have their baby, all this comes to an abrupt halt, and the surrogate may experience depression.

"All of this is experienced without her baby. Now, a surrogate can get treatment for depression, but Mrs. Loman was all alone in Elk Grove with no support system, and this led to her paranoid state."

"Did Mrs. Loman experience paranoid delusions?"

"Definitely. She told several people that the Lindstroms, the Elk Grove hospital, her lawyer, and others were in a conspiracy to steal her baby, whose name is Roy, but who she calls Peter."

"Does she acknowledge that she signed away her parental rights?"

"Yes, but she claims this was part of a plot. She insists that the contract is illegal and that you can't sell a baby. She has told me that she believes that she may have been drugged or hypnotized when she signed the contract."

"Was there a triggering event that led Mrs. Loman to take the Lindstroms' baby?"

"The stress and anxiety coupled with the changes in the surrogate's body can make them see threats everywhere. In Mrs. Loman's case, she believed that there were two men who had come to Elk Grove to kill her. She believed that she had to run from them. She had hired a lawyer and filed a lawsuit to get custody of Roy, but she was impelled to take him from the

Lindstroms immediately when her paranoia led her to believe that she would be killed if she stayed in Elk Grove."

"In our state," Robin said, "a person is not responsible for criminal conduct if, at the time of the conduct as a result of a mental disease or defect, she lacks the substantial capacity either to appreciate the criminality of her conduct or to conform her conduct to the requirements of law. In your medical opinion, is Marjorie Loman suffering from a mental disease?"

"Most definitely."

"When she took the Lindstroms' baby, did she appreciate the criminality of her act?"

"No. In my opinion as a medical doctor, Mrs. Lindstrom was existing in a parallel mental universe where the baby was hers and the Lindstroms, the Elk Grove hospital, her lawyer, and the police were part of a conspiracy to steal her baby from her. Furthermore, she honestly believed that two killers were after her, so she couldn't wait for her lawsuit to go to trial and had to act immediately if she ever wanted to get her baby."

"No further questions, Your Honor," Robin said.

"Mr. Hatcher."

"Thank you, Your Honor." He turned to the witness stand. "Dr. Suarez, isn't it true that postpartum psychosis can lead a birth mother to subject her baby to extreme violence?"

"Yes."

"Isn't it a fact that mothers suffering from postpartum psychosis have murdered their children?"

"Yes."

"Are you aware of a Texas case where a mother drowned her five children or the California woman who drowned her infant son because she believed he was possessed by the devil?"

"Yes."

"So, it's not inconceivable, is it, that the defendant subjected Roy to violence while she had him?"

"It's not inconceivable, but it doesn't jibe with the facts of this case. According to Dr. Lancaster, the baby was not abused."

"Did you read the testimony of Dr. Wolfe?"

"I did."

"If she's right, the defendant became angry or frustrated and subjected baby Roy to the type of violence other mothers with postpartum psychosis have inflicted on their children."

"If she's right, but I've looked at the evidence of alleged abuse, and I find that Dr. Lancaster's explanation fits the facts much better than Dr. Wolfe's."

"You want this jury to believe that Mrs. Loman is crazy, don't you?"

"I want the jurors to accept my diagnosis of postpartum psychosis as an explanation for Mrs. Loman's actions."

"Isn't the fact that Mrs. Loman hired an attorney to

sue for custody of baby Roy evidence that she was acting rationally?"

"It depends on her motivation. If she hired an attorney to gain custody of baby Roy because she believed that there was a wide-ranging conspiracy to steal her child, I would say that the basis of her action was irrational."

"No further questions," Hatcher said when he accepted the fact that he wasn't going to make any headway with Dr. Suarez.

"Mr. McDermott, do you have another witness?" Judge Stonehouse asked.

"No, Your Honor. The defense rests."

"Do you have any rebuttal witnesses, Mr. Hatcher?" Judge Stonehouse asked the prosecutor.

"No, Your Honor."

"Then I'll dismiss the jury for today, and I'll meet with you and the defense attorneys after lunch to discuss the jury instructions. We'll reconvene in the morning for the closing arguments."

Stan and Robin escorted Dr. Suarez through the gauntlet the reporters had set up and rushed her outside the courthouse to the car that was waiting to take her to the airport.

"What do you think?" Stan asked Robin when they were free of the mob and headed back to Stan's office to work on his closing argument.

"Suarez was terrific, and I don't think Hatcher scored many points on cross. When I get home, I'll ask my mother how she and my sisters-in-law are leaning. I think they'll be a good indicator of how well or badly we're doing."

"Have you already asked her what the gang thinks?"

Robin nodded. "After Dr. Lancaster testified."

"And?"

"Three out of four would have acquitted on the child abuse charge, but they all thought Marjorie should go down for hitting Emily Lindstrom and kidnapping the baby."

"It will be interesting to hear their opinion now that Dr. Suarez has testified, but don't tell me how they'd vote until after I argue," Stan said with a smile. "I'll just get depressed if I think the assault and kidnapping are a lost cause."

CHAPTER THIRTY

"Your closing argument, Mr. Hatcher," Judge Stonehouse said when court reconvened.

The prosecutor walked to the jury box and paused for dramatic effect.

"I want to thank you for the attention you've paid during a trial that could not have been a pleasant experience. It is one thing to learn that an adult has been injured, but it is far worse to hear about abuse suffered by a defenseless infant. And make no mistake; Roy Lindstrom suffered abuse at the hands of Marjorie Loman, who pistol-whipped the baby's legal mother before stealing her child from her.

"This is a simple case. The judge will instruct you on the legal definitions of kidnapping and assault, but basically, kidnapping occurs when a defendant seizes and carries away a person by force, and assault occurs when a defendant inflicts physical harm on a person. It should be pretty clear that shaking Roy Lindstrom hard enough to cause injury to his brain and hitting Emily Lindstrom on the head with a heavy pistol are assaults, and that stealing the Lindstroms' baby and going on the run with him is kidnapping.

"The defense has tried to muddy the waters by calling in a professor from a big medical school to argue that Dr. Nadine Wolfe doesn't know what she's talking about when she used the shaken baby syndrome to diagnose abuse. But even the professor had to admit that the majority of medical professionals agree that shaken baby syndrome and abusive head trauma are valid bases for a diagnosis of abuse. And let's not forget that Dr. Lancaster wasn't in the emergency room when baby Roy was brought in. He never held the baby. All he held were x-rays and pieces of paper.

"Then we have another doctor from out of state, who comes in to make excuses for the defendant's terrible actions. Poor Mrs. Loman hit Emily Lindstrom in the head because she was afraid of two mythical killers and had to save her baby from a conspiracy.

"Let's think about that. Mrs. Loman spent an evening nurturing baby Roy, and that gave her second thoughts about the contract she'd signed and received thousands of dollars for fulfilling. She isn't nuts. Hiring a lawyer to sue to get the child back is a very rational act. Even if she was depressed because she regretted giving up baby Roy, feeling blue is not an excuse for pistol-whipping a defenseless woman or subjecting an innocent baby to violent shaking.

"Don't be distracted by the theories of the defense witnesses, none of whom were in Elk Grove when these crimes occurred. Put your faith in the doctor who actually saw baby Roy after he was rescued from the woman who kidnapped and abused him.

"After you've calmly assessed all the evidence of violence and abuse that we have shown you, I think you will conclude beyond a reasonable doubt that the defendant intentionally assaulted Emily Lindstrom and kidnapped and assaulted baby Roy Lindstrom. Thank you."

Stan was right, Robin thought. *Hatcher is an excellent attorney, and that was a dynamite closing argument.* But she kept her thoughts to herself, because she didn't want to bring Stan down. Instead, she whispered, "Go get 'em," as Stan rose and walked to the jury box.

"Baby Roy is just fine. He was fine when he was taken to the emergency room from the Prairie Lodge motel, he was fine when he left King City General Hospital, and you heard Emily Lindstrom tell you that he is fine today. If Marjorie Loman shook Roy hard enough to cause brain damage, he would not be okay.

"No disrespect to Dr. Wolfe, but her expertise is in emergency medicine. She is not an expert in diagnosing a baby's medical problems. Pediatricians do that. If you need proof, go no further than her misdiagnosing Mongolian spots as bruises caused by abuse or calling the minimal retinal hemorrhages a part of the triad of the shaken baby syndrome.

"Before you can find Marjorie guilty of abusing Roy Lindstrom, the State has to prove the abuse occurred to the point where you have no reasonable doubts in your mind about the truth of the charge. That is a very, very high standard, because, in our American system of justice, we dread the thought of sending an innocent person to prison.

"When you start deliberating in the jury room, if in your mind, intellectually, you are pretty sure Marjorie is guilty, and in your heart, emotionally, you are pretty sure she has committed a crime, but something you saw or heard during the trial makes you stop and say, 'I'm pretty sure she did it, but this makes me wonder if I am wrong,' the judge will tell you that it is your patriotic duty as an American citizen to bring in a verdict of not guilty.

"I submit that there are many things you heard in this trial that should raise reasonable doubts. First, on the abuse charge, Mr. Hatcher has tried to use an old tactic by belittling an eminent professor of medicine because he doesn't live in Elk Grove. What you should consider is the prestigious position he holds and his qualifications in the field that is central to the State's case.

"Dr. Lancaster explained that the shaken baby theory was never intended to be used in criminal cases when it was thought up. It was supposed to be used to educate parents and doctors about the problems some doctors thought were caused by shaking babies. But it has never been tested, and it shouldn't be used in criminal cases.

"Now, Dr. Wolfe laughed at the suggestion that we test the hypothesis by violently shaking thousands of babies to see if they develop the triad. I agree. The idea is ridiculous and criminal. But that creates a problem for Mr. Hatcher. Before scientists and doctors accept a hypothesis as true, they test it. If you don't test it, you shouldn't accept it as true.

"If I told you that I had an idea that eating hot dogs cured cancer, would you stop your doctor's suggested treatments and start eating hot dogs if I couldn't produce the results of clinical studies that proved my hypothesis? Of course you wouldn't.

"You've also heard that no biomechanical test has ever produced the force necessary to cause the damage that shaking is supposed to produce, and that commissions in Canada and England and a Wisconsin court have suggested that the syndrome should not be used to convict a person of abuse.

"So, let's return to the beyond-a-reasonable-doubt standard. If you accept Dr. Lancaster's testimony, you would have a reasonable doubt that Marjorie abused Roy Lindstrom. But you also have to acquit if you aren't sure who is right and who is wrong.

"On top of that, the fact that Roy is a healthy, happy baby today should make you doubt Dr. Wolfe's conclusions. So, I submit that the evidence taken as a whole raises serious, reasonable doubts about the ability of the State to prove the charge of child abuse.

"Let's move to the charges of assault on Emily Lindstrom and the kidnapping of Roy Lindstrom. There is no question that Marjorie struck Emily with a gun and took Roy. What is in question is why she committed these acts.

"Judge Stonehouse is going to instruct you that in our state, a person is not responsible for criminal conduct if at the time of the conduct, as a result of a mental disease or defect, she lacks the substantial capacity either to appreciate the criminality of her conduct or to conform her conduct to the requirements of law.

"Dr. Gabrielle Suarez explained that healthy women can suffer a terrible mental disease called *postpartum psychosis* after giving birth, and that the problems of being separated from her child, having her daily routine ended, and not having a support system can make this medical problem worse when the mother is a surrogate.

"How did Nurse Cleary describe Marjorie's reaction when she learned that she would never see the baby she carried inside her for nine months ever again? She said that Marjorie howled like an animal that has had her cub torn from her.

"How would you describe Marjorie's actions after she gave birth? Were they the actions of a sane person? She calls the baby Peter, when his name is Roy. She goes to the Lindstroms' house and screams and threatens. She tells people that there is a conspiracy to take her baby. Who is in this conspiracy? The conspirators are her lawyer, the hospital, the Lindstroms, the police. And then there are the two killers. Isn't this belief that literally everyone is plotting against her and that she is being pursued by killers a clear sign that Marjorie is suffering from a severe mental disease that has her living in an alternate universe?

"I started my closing argument by telling you that baby Roy is fine. I'll end it by telling you that Marjorie Loman is not fine. After Marjorie gave birth, the hospital made a terrible mistake and allowed her to bond with her baby. Then they took the baby from her and caused the onset of a terrible mental disease. Marjorie is suffering from postpartum psychosis. Dr. Suarez told you that it is her opinion as an eminent psychiatrist who specializes in the psychiatric problems of mothers that Marjorie lacks the substantial capacity to appreciate the criminality of her conduct.

"Mr. Hatcher has not called any doctor, psychiatrist, or expert to contradict Dr. Suarez's conclusion. So, you are left with the uncontested conclusion that, sadly, Marjorie Loman was suffering from a serious mental illness when she hit Emily Lindstrom, who she believed was part of a conspiracy to steal her son, and ran away with a baby she was convinced had been stolen from her. Thank you."

When Stan sat down, Marjorie gripped his forearm. "Thank you," she whispered as tears ran down her cheeks. Stan put his arm around her shoulder. Robin saw the jurors watching.

"That was terrific," Robin whispered to Stan.

Hatcher stood and walked to the jury box. This was his last chance to convince the jurors to convict, but Robin didn't think his rebuttal was as effective as his initial closing argument. She thought that he should have ignored the accusation that he had not produced an expert to counter Dr. Suarez, but he chose to argue that the doctor's testimony wasn't worthy of belief and that Marjorie's actions were logical and rational.

Robin also thought that Hatcher's flailing efforts to counter the argument that the jurors should have a reasonable doubt if they couldn't decide between the testimony of Dr. Wolfe and Dr. Lancaster were especially damaging to the prosecution's case.

After Hatcher was finished, Judge Stonehouse instructed the jury and sent them to deliberate before recessing court. Hatcher left quickly so he could talk to the reporters who were waiting for him outside the courtroom.

"What's going to happen to me?" Marjorie asked.

"I thought our experts were great, and Stan gave a dynamite closing," Robin said, "but I learned long ago that it's useless to try to predict what a jury will do. So, hang tough, and let's hope everything works out."

The guards escorted Marjorie back to the jail, and Robin and Stan gathered their files.

"I predict a long wait for a verdict," Stan said. "Do you want to go to Lee's for lunch?"

"Sure," Robin said, although she never had much of an appetite while a jury was out.

"You were fantastic," Stan said as he and Robin walked to Lee's.

"Dr. Suarez and Dr. Lancaster were fantastic. I just asked the questions."

"Don't get modest on me. I would never have thought about a postpartum psychosis defense. If Marjorie walks, it will be because of you."

Stan's praise made Robin very uncomfortable. She and Stan had spent every waking hour together since she'd come back to Elk Grove for the trial, and she could not deny that she was attracted to him, but the emotions she experienced because Jeff had been taken from her were still raw. Feeling an attraction to any man just didn't feel right.

CHAPTER THIRTY-ONE

When no verdict had been reached by six o'clock, Judge Stonehouse had dinner sent into the jury room. The judge checked again at nine and sent the jurors home when they told him that they were still deliberating.

Robin spent the night tossing and turning, and her morning run didn't sweep away the cobwebs. Mark had sent Robin the transcripts in a case on appeal to the Oregon Supreme Court. She worked on the brief while she waited for word that Marjorie's fate had been decided, but she had to force herself to concentrate. A little after eleven, Stan opened her office door and told Robin that the jury had reached a verdict.

Neither lawyer said a word as they walked to the courthouse with Stan's associates trailing behind.

A herd of reporters dogged the defense team as they walked to the courtroom, refusing to take Stan's "No comment" as an answer.

When she walked into the courtroom, Robin saw Roger Dillon and his partner, Carrie Anders, sitting in the back row on the aisle.

"Give me a minute," she told Stan. "I need to talk to someone."

Stan frowned, but he saw the guards leading Marjorie to the counsel table, and he went to meet her.

"What are you two doing here?" Robin asked.

Carrie smiled. "Aren't you glad to see old friends?"

"I'm guessing I won't be," she replied. "Is this about the murder charge?"

Roger nodded. "We're here to transport Mrs. Loman to Portland if she's acquitted."

Robin was about to say something when the bailiff called the court to order.

"Let's talk later," she said. Then she hurried down the aisle and through the bar of the court. On her way, she saw her mother and sisters-in-law in the middle row and the Lindstroms sitting behind Rodney Hatcher.

Moments after Robin took her seat, the jury filed in. Robin noted that they looked grim, and only a few of the jurors cast glances in the direction of either of the parties.

"Good afternoon," Judge Stonehouse said to the jurors. "I understand you've arrived at a verdict."

Alex Mulberry, a retired schoolteacher, stood. He held several papers in his hands. "We have, Your Honor."

"Please stand, Mrs. Loman," the judge instructed. Marjorie and her lawyers stood up. Stan and Robin looked at Alex Mulberry, but Marjorie looked at the floor.

"Can I take it that you are the foreperson, Mr. Mulberry?"

"Yes, sir."

"Okay, then. How do you find on count one in the indictment that charges Mrs. Loman with assaulting Roy Lindstrom?"

"We find her not guilty."

Marjorie sagged, and an audible murmur coursed through the spectator section. The judge rapped his gavel and told the spectators to quiet down.

"Mr. Mulberry, how does the jury find the defendant on count two of the indictment, which charges her with assaulting Emily Lindstrom?"

Mulberry cleared his throat before telling the judge that the jury had found Marjorie not guilty. Marjorie began to weep, and Stan and Robin were comforting her when the jury foreperson told Judge Stonehouse that the jury had found Marjorie not guilty of kidnapping Roy Lindstrom.

There was an audible gasp from the Lindstroms. Robin turned her head and saw Rodney Hatcher staring at the jury in disbelief. She had no urge to smile and no interest in gloating. Robin respected the effort that Hatcher had put into prosecuting a very serious case that could easily have gone his way.

Marjorie collapsed on her chair, and Stan wrapped an arm around her shoulder as she wept.

"It's okay," he told her. "It's all over."

But Robin saw the Portland detectives walking down the aisle toward the front of the court and knew that Marjorie Loman's real ordeal was just starting.

Marjorie saw where Robin was looking. Her expression changed from relief over the verdict to fright. "What are they doing here?" she asked.

"You know them?" Robin said.

"They're the detectives who came to my house and told me that Joel had been killed."

Robin put a hand on Marjorie's shoulder. "I want you to stay calm."

"Why? What's going to happen?"

"There's a warrant for your arrest for your husband's murder. Those detectives are here to take you back to Portland."

Marjorie's hand flew to her chest. "Oh, God. No. You have to protect me."

"I can't stop them from taking you back, but I know these detectives. They're straight shooters. I'm going to tell them I'm your lawyer and that they can't question you. I'll be back in Portland in two days. I'll talk to you then. Meanwhile, do not discuss the case with anyone. Do you understand?"

"I was a cop, Robin. I know the drill."

Robin put her hand on Marjorie's shoulder and gave it a gentle squeeze. "I know this is awful after what you've just gone through, but hang in there. Stan and I got you out of one scrape. Hopefully, I'll get you out of another."

CHAPTER THIRTY-TWO

"This is bullshit," Stan fumed as he walked back to his office at a furious pace.

"We knew this could happen as soon as Oregon served the warrant. The hold was one of the reasons Judge Stonehouse denied bail."

"Are you going to represent Marjorie in Oregon?" Stan asked.

"Probably. I want to talk to her in Portland before I decide."

"Hatcher is behind this," Stan said angrily. "He hates to lose."

"Don't blame Hatcher. The authorities in Portland knew she was here."

Stan's shoulders sagged, and he slowed his pace.

"You're right. It just seems so unfair after she went through this ordeal."

"I know you're upset, but Marjorie did pistol-whip Emily, and she did kidnap Roy. The jury could just as easily have convicted on all or some of the counts."

Stan shook his head. "How can you be so cold and objective?"

"I couldn't do my job if I got emotionally involved with a client."

"I guess that's what you have to do when you handle the blood-and-guts cases you take on in Portland. Me, I know everyone in this town, so every case is personal."

Robin smiled. "That's why you'll get an ulcer before I do, and I'll become an alcoholic."

Stan laughed. "You are amazing, Robin."

"No, I'm just a conscientious attorney. And you fit that definition too."

"And together, we made a great team."

"I agree."

Stan stopped walking. He looked nervous. Robin knew what was coming, and she'd dreaded the moment.

"When are you headed back to Portland?" Stan asked.

"I've got a flight out late tomorrow."

"I'm going to miss you." Stan paused and took a

deep breath. "Look," he said, "I know what you've been through—why you came back to Elk Grove. And I know I shouldn't be saying this, but you'll be gone tomorrow, so I won't get another chance. What I want to say is, if there comes a time when you decide you want to take another chance on someone . . ."

Robin reached out and touched Stan's arm. "I think you're a terrific person and a terrific lawyer, but my heart is just empty now, and I'm too sad and lost to think about the future."

"I get that, and I know it's way too soon after losing someone you loved so much," Stan said. "Just keep me in the back of your mind, and stay in touch."

"I will, and if you get another crazy case, give me a call."

"Deal. So, how about one more meal at Lee's?"

Lunch had been awkward, and Robin steered the conversation into safe waters by talking sports and politics. After lunch, Robin cleaned out her office and said goodbye to Stan and his associates. Then she headed home, where she found Shirley watching television in the living room. Her mother turned off the set as soon as she heard the front door open.

"Are you hungry?" Shirley asked.

"Stan and I had lunch at Lee's."

"You two did a good job."

"Thanks."

"Of course, we were surprised that the Loman woman got off scot-free."

"Oh?"

"We were all sure that the jury would convict her for hitting Emily Lindstrom and kidnapping the baby."

"They must have accepted Dr. Suarez's testimony and decided that she was mentally ill when she went to the Lindstroms' house."

"I guess they must have. I wouldn't, and neither would the girls," Shirley said in a stern voice.

Robin laughed. "Then I'm glad you weren't on the jury."

"When you were defending her, did you know that she murdered her husband in Oregon?" Shirley asked.

"Marjorie is *charged* with murdering her husband, and she says she didn't. And yes, I knew about the indictment. How did you know about it?"

"Everybody knows. It's all over the local news."

"Then I'm glad I'm not trying the murder case in Elk Grove. I'd have a tough time finding twelve unbiased jurors."

"Are you representing her in Oregon?"

"She's asked me to."

"Hmm."

"What's that mean?"

"Nothing. So, it looked like you and Stan got along pretty well."

"We did. He's a good lawyer."

"They say his firm is doing quite well."

"Any chance we can have everyone over for dinner tomorrow before I fly home?" Robin asked to divert her mother's attention from her plans for Robin's marriage to Stan McDermott.

"That's already taken care of. We're all going to Jack's at four."

Robin walked over and hugged her mother. "It's been great seeing you and my brothers again."

"Try not to wait so long."

"I won't. What were you watching when I came in?" Robin asked.

"Another *Perry Mason.* They're on at midnight, so I tape them."

"Mind if I join you?"

"Not a bit."

"Who is Perry representing now?"

"This priest heard a murderer's confession, and he asked Perry to tell him if he should go to the police."

"I think there's a priest-penitent privilege, but I'm not sure," Robin said.

"Do you think the priest will be murdered?" Shirley asked. She sounded concerned.

"I don't know. We'll just have to wait and see."

PART FIVE

THE TWO-KILLER DEFENSE

CHAPTER THIRTY-THREE

Robin's flight landed in Portland a little before eleven at night, and she took a Lyft from the airport to her condo. It was dark in the apartment, and Robin didn't turn on the lights. She set her bag down and sat on the sofa in the living room. The night cloaked the mountains in darkness, but there were scattered lights in the buildings across the way. Robin wondered about the people who lived in those apartments. Were their lives peaceful, or were they as tumultuous as the life she was living?

Robin closed her eyes and thought about the past forty-eight hours. There had been the farewell dinner at Jack's house—a raucous affair like all the Lockwood dinners, with screaming, laughing children, her combative brothers arguing about everything, her sisters-in-law chatting peacefully, oblivious to the chaos, and Shirley, the matriarch, firmly in charge. Robin hadn't realized how hard it would be to say goodbye. They had all been there for her when she needed them, and she vowed to return to Elk Grove more often.

Then there was Stan McDermott. He was right when he said that they made a great team, and she believed that something might have happened if they'd met before she'd fallen in love with Jeff. She knew that nothing would ever happen between them now. She wasn't going to trade her exciting law practice in Portland, a city she loved, for Stan's sleepy general practice in a small town she'd been eager to leave, and Stan would never leave Elk Grove and move to Oregon.

More important, no matter how much she liked Stan, she didn't feel the same overpowering emotions she'd felt when she was with Jeff. When she was near Jeff, she felt like she was floating. Just seeing him brought a smile to her face. She didn't know if she would ever feel that way again, but she knew Stan didn't make her feel that way.

Finally, she thought about Marjorie Loman, whose emotions had gone from sky high when she was found not guilty of abusing the baby she loved, to deep depression when she was told that she would have to go through the ordeal of a murder trial in Oregon. Robin couldn't imagine how Marjorie must feel, sitting in another cell in another city.

Robin's eyes were closing, and she forced herself to stand up. She carried her bag into the bedroom, but she didn't have enough energy to unpack. Minutes later, she threw the covers over her and passed out.

Robin wanted to sleep late, but her brain was still in Elk Grove, where it was two hours later. She tried to will herself back to dreamland. The effort failed, so she put on her workout gear and ran to McGill's gym.

Robin felt like she was moving through mud during her workout, and she was still sluggish and exhausted when she walked to her office. On the way, she stopped for a latte in hopes that the caffeine would defog her brain, but it only helped a little.

Mark Berman had just said goodbye to a client when Robin walked into the reception area of Barrister, Berman, and Lockwood.

"We're going to have to start calling you the *Little Sorceress,* after the rabbit you pulled out of a hat in Elk Grove," Mark joked.

Regina Barrister, the firm's founder, had been called the *Sorceress* because of her uncanny ability to win seemingly unwinnable cases.

"Marjorie's troubles aren't over," Robin said. "Roger Dillon and Carrie Anders were in the courtroom when the verdict came in, and they arrested her on a warrant that charges her with murdering her husband."

"Are you going to represent her?"

"I'll decide after we talk this afternoon. There are a few things I need to know before I'll agree to be Marjorie's lawyer."

Robin spent the rest of the morning in her office going through her snail mail and emails and editing a brief that Loretta Washington had drafted.

After lunch, Robin went to the Justice Center, an eighteen-story, concrete-and-steel building in downtown Portland that housed the Multnomah County jail on its fourth through tenth floors. Robin walked into the building's vaulted lobby, passed a curving staircase that led to the courtrooms on the next floor, and through a set of glass doors that opened into the jail reception area. Robin showed her ID to the duty officer and went through a metal detector before taking the elevator to the floor with the contact visiting rooms.

A guard escorted Robin to the room that had been set aside for her meeting with Marjorie Loman. As soon as she saw the room, Robin stopped and leaned against the concrete wall. Her heart was tripping, and she felt faint. It was the same room where she'd had her initial contact with Lloyd Arness.

"Are you okay?" the guard asked, concerned by Robin's waxy pallor.

"Just a little jet-lagged," she lied. "I flew into town

late yesterday, and I got up too early." Robin took a deep breath and straightened up. "I'm okay now."

"You know you can ring for me if you need to," the guard said.

"Thanks. You're very considerate. I'm sure I'll be okay."

It was a few minutes before another guard ushered Marjorie Loman into the contact visiting room. The delay gave Robin time to compose herself.

Marjorie looked like a zombie. Weeks in the sun-deprived confines of a jail cell had leached the color from her skin, and the speed with which she had gone from elation after her acquittal to the horror of a murder charge had sapped her spirit.

"We have to stop meeting like this," Robin said in a lame attempt to lighten the atmosphere in the depressing concrete room.

Marjorie forced a smile. "Get me out of here, and I'll meet you anywhere you want."

"I'm going to try, but there are a few things I've got to know before I agree to represent you."

"I can pay you. I still have money from the sale of my house and the penthouse."

"It's not that. I need to know about the baby. Are you going to try to take Roy from the Lindstroms?" Robin asked, using the name the Lindstroms had bestowed on their son to see how Marjorie would react.

Marjorie looked down at the top of the metal table that separated her from Robin. "I've had a lot of time to think in jail. I'm going to drop the lawsuit. I've accepted the fact that Emily and Caleb are Peter's legal parents."

"His name isn't Peter, and the fact that you're still calling him Peter really worries me," Robin said.

"I'm always going to think of my baby as Peter, but you don't have to worry. I'm never going back to Elk Grove, and I'll never bother the Lindstroms again."

"If you want me to be your lawyer, you've got to do more than promise. You have to convince me that you won't go after the Lindstroms' child."

Marjorie looked at Robin. "I was mentally ill when I kidnapped Peter and took him on the run. Now that I've had time to think about what I did, I know that's no way to raise a child. How would he grow up and be normal? I love Peter, but I know that the Lindstroms love him too. They can raise him in a stable, loving home. My life is a mess right now. Even if a jury clears me on this charge, I'll still be a pariah. I won't subject a child to living with a single mother who will always be known as a murderer and child abuser."

Robin stared into Marjorie's eyes for a moment. Then she nodded. "Okay. Tell me why the police think you murdered your husband."

"When the detectives came to our house to tell me Joel was dead, I told them that I hated him, but I didn't kill him. And if I did, I would never have tortured him. I just couldn't do that. But hating Joel gives me a motive. And then there's the gold. Joel was a complete bastard. As soon as he decided to divorce me, he drained our bank accounts and converted most of it into gold. I'm not sure of the exact amount, but it's in the millions. Now that Joel is dead, the gold is mine because I'm his widow. All I have to do is claim it."

"Several million dollars in gold does give you a powerful motive for murder."

"That it does, but there's a problem."

"Oh?"

"No one, including Joel's lawyer, knows where the gold is. It could be in any country in the world."

"Other than motive, do you know why the police think you murdered Joel?"

Marjorie shrugged. "Maybe it's because I ran away and used an alias. That would have made me look guilty."

"Why did you run?"

"I told you in Elk Grove. The same day those detectives told me that Joel had been murdered, these two men showed up at my door and told me that Joel owed their boss a quarter of a million dollars and that it was my debt now that Joel was dead. They never came out and said that they'd murdered Joel, but they implied that they had. When they followed me to Elk Grove, I knew I had to run again."

"The two men were real?" Robin asked.

Marjorie nodded. "The day I took Peter, I saw them knocking on the door to my apartment in Elk Grove. I took their picture. I still have it on my phone. I can show it to you."

"When we were in Elk Grove, why didn't you tell Stan and me that you had a picture of these men that would prove they existed?"

"You, McDermott, and Dr. Suarez thought they were a figment of my imagination. I didn't try to disabuse you of that belief because I knew it would help my insanity defense. But they are real."

Robin frowned. If Marjorie was wise enough to know that an acquittal on the kidnapping and assault charges depended on her convincing everyone that the two men were a figment of her imagination, then the whole postpartum psychosis defense might have been a sham.

"Can you think of another reason the DA is going after you? There has to be more than motives and the fact that you ran. Can you think of any hard evidence that connects you to the murder?"

"If there is, I'm as much in the dark as you are."

CHAPTER THIRTY-FOUR

When Robin walked into Vanessa Cole's office, the Multnomah County district attorney walked around her desk and hugged her. Robin was embarrassed, but she didn't pull away. After a moment, Vanessa pushed Robin to arm's length, but kept her hands on her adversary's shoulders.

"How are you doing?" Vanessa asked.

"I'm okay," Robin answered, but Vanessa could see that she wasn't. She squeezed Robin's shoulders and walked back to her chair. Robin took a seat.

"Carrie and Roger told me that they saw you in Elk Grove. They didn't think that there were many attorneys who could have wrestled a not-guilty verdict out of a jury, given what they knew about the case."

Robin blushed. "It wasn't just me, Vanessa. I had an excellent cocounsel and dynamite expert witnesses."

"I assume you've come to tell me that you're representing Mrs. Loman on the murder charge."

Robin nodded.

"Carrie said that Loman came across as a sympathetic defendant in Elk Grove. She won't here. And don't think I'm going to cut you any slack because I gave you that hug."

Robin smiled. "Damn. I was hoping you'd gone soft."

"Not a chance."

"What makes you think Marjorie killed her husband?"

"I'll send over the discovery this afternoon and you can see for yourself, but I'll give you the highlights. We've got motive galore. There's the divorce, which was really vicious. Your client laughed when Carrie and Roger told Mrs. Loman that her husband had been murdered and tortured. Then there's the money; millions from what Joel's lawyer told us. I assume you know that Joel cleaned out their accounts, converted it to gold, and hid it."

"Go on."

"Then there's the blood and the DNA."

Robin frowned. "I'm not sure I know what you mean."

"It's in the reports. We executed a search warrant

for your client's house and a car that Joel leased that was abandoned at the airport. The lab found DNA, blood, and hair in the trunk of the car. The DNA was from your client and her husband. We also found Joel's blood in the entryway of the Lomans' home. Your client worked hard to hide the traces, but she didn't get it all."

When Robin returned to her office, she was nowhere near as confident about Marjorie's case as she'd been when she walked into Vanessa's office. Marjorie had a lot of explaining to do, but Robin didn't want to confront her until she'd gone through the discovery.

"Mark wants to see you," the receptionist said as soon as Robin walked into the waiting room.

When Robin knocked on Mark's doorjamb, he looked up from the contract he was reviewing.

"You wanted to see me?"

"Yeah. Do you have a minute?" Mark asked.

"Sure."

Mark looked uncomfortable. "I didn't want to bring this up before the Elk Grove trial, but I don't think we can put it off any longer. I know this is going to upset you, but the firm needs an investigator." Mark saw the color drain from his partner's face. "Are you okay?"

"Not really, but you're right. I'll need someone to work Marjorie Loman's case."

"And I need someone on two of mine. I started interviewing while you were away, and I have a few possibilities, but there's one person who stood out."

"Who is it?"

Mark handed Robin a stack of résumés. "Look through these and see who you think is the most interesting."

Mark turned back to the contract while Robin read through the résumés. Twenty minutes later, she looked up. "Ken Breland?" she asked.

Mark smiled. "Great minds think alike."

"Have you interviewed him?"

Mark nodded.

Robin held up the résumé. "So, this is real?"

Mark nodded. "I checked his references as much as they could be checked. He was a Navy SEAL and CIA. I asked him what he did in those jobs. He was pretty blunt. He said most of what he did was classified, and he hoped not being able to talk about it wouldn't hurt his chances of getting the job."

"How did you learn about him?" Robin asked.

"Your buddy Carrie Anders called while you were in Elk Grove. Breland's in his late fifties. He was married, but his wife passed away five years ago, shortly before he retired from the CIA. He told me that he got tired of playing golf, so he volunteered to work on cold cases for the Portland PD. Carrie said that the guy is very, very good and they'd hate to lose him, but she told him about Jeff and he said that he'd be interested in the job."

"Why don't you set up an interview and I'll see what I think, but he sounds almost too good to be true."

CHAPTER THIRTY-FIVE

"We have to talk," Robin told Marjorie Loman as soon as they were alone in the contact visiting room.

Marjorie could see that Robin was upset, and that made her nervous. "Did something happen?" she asked.

"Yeah, Marjorie, you could say that. I read the report of the police investigation in your case. Can you think of any reason why the police found Joel's blood in the entryway of your house and his blood and hair and your DNA in the trunk of Joel's Mercedes, which was abandoned in the parking lot of the Portland airport?"

"That was Joel's car, so that would explain his hair and DNA. He used it for business."

"Do you think the jurors will buy the argument that

he liked to cut his hair in his car trunk and nicked himself when he was shaving?"

Marjorie's temper flared. "What, suddenly you think I'm a killer?"

"Suddenly, I'm thinking you haven't been straight with me. The blood, the hair, and the DNA can send you to prison for life or worse unless you can give me an explanation I can serve up to a jury of your peers."

Marjorie broke eye contact and looked down at the tabletop.

"You're a cop, so you know enough law to know that anything you tell me is confidential," Robin said. "I can't tell a soul what you tell me, but I can't defend you if you keep secrets."

Marjorie continued to stare at the top of the metal table. Robin knew that one of the best ways to get someone to talk was to stop asking questions, so she leaned back in her chair, stared at Marjorie, and waited.

The silence in the room grew. Then Marjorie sighed. "This is bad," she said.

"Did you kill Joel?"

Marjorie's head jerked up. "No. I never hurt him, but I did get rid of his body."

"Explain that to me."

"The day before Joel's body was discovered in Portland, I came home from my shift and found his body in the entryway. The Mercedes was parked in the turnaround. I was certain that I'd been set up, and the police were on the way."

"What did you do when you found the body?"

"I loaded Joel in the trunk of the Mercedes and drove to Portland so he wouldn't be discovered anywhere near our house. Once I got rid of the body, I tried as hard as I could to get rid of the blood, but it was dark and I was in a panic, and obviously, I didn't get it all. Then I drove the Mercedes to the airport and abandoned it." Marjorie looked directly at her lawyer. "Do you believe me?"

"I don't have to believe you to defend you, but the jurors do if you testify. Your explanation may be hard for them to swallow."

Marjorie leaned across the table and fixed Robin with a determined stare. "What I just told you is the truth."

"Who did you think was trying to frame you for the murder?"

"Joel used the Mercedes for business, and he'd been screwing Kelly Starrett, his partner. Joel embezzled millions from his firm. Enough to sink it. What if Starrett found out that the firm was broke because Joel embezzled the money? Kelly would be able to get the car if it was parked at their office. She's furious, so she kills him and leaves the body in my entryway to frame me. That could be what happened."

"Is Starrett strong enough to overpower Joel?"

"Joel was a lightweight. Kelly is big. She pumps iron and runs marathons. She's strong enough to overpower Joel and put the body in the trunk of the car."

"Starrett's DNA was found in the Mercedes, and a blond hair was also in the trunk," Robin said. "Is she a blonde?"

"She is. And we have two other suspects that can raise a reasonable doubt with the jury."

"Who are they?"

"The two thugs who threatened me after the body was found. The police never came to my house until after Joel's body was discovered. Do you see what that means?"

"Explain it to me."

"If those men killed Joel, they didn't leave him in the house to frame me. If that's what they wanted to do, they would have called the police, but they didn't do that.

"If they killed Joel, he must not have broken when they tortured him. He must have died before he told them where he hid the gold. That's why they left the body in our house. They wanted to scare me into telling them where the gold was hidden, only I don't know where it is. That's why I took off."

Robin's head was starting to hurt from considering all the possibilities, and she was still jet-lagged. "I think this is enough for today. I'm going back to my office to think about what you've told me. It's a lot to digest."

Robin was confused when she left the jail. Marjorie's explanations made sense, but she had been so eager to have Robin jump on the Starrett or the two-killer bandwagon that Robin's suspicions were aroused.

Robin didn't have to believe Marjorie to defend her. The State had the burden of proving beyond a reasonable doubt that Marjorie had murdered her husband. From the viewpoint of the defense, her guilt or innocence was irrelevant when they were in a courtroom. But Robin always felt more comfortable if she was convinced that her client was innocent. She was on the fence in Marjorie's case, and she knew she wouldn't sleep soundly if she thought that her client was conning her.

Of course, a juror who was as undecided as Robin had to acquit, so they would win if Robin could convince the jurors that Starrett or the two men might have killed Joel.

A sudden rush of adrenaline stopped Robin in her tracks. Traffic sped by and people passed her, but she was oblivious to her surroundings. An idea had burst in on her like a cerebral SWAT team.

CHAPTER THIRTY-SIX

Robin and Jeff loved the 1940s, black-and-white, tough-guy detective movies like *The Big Sleep* and *The Maltese Falcon,* and she had a mental picture of Ken Breland as a modern-day Humphrey Bogart—a world-weary gumshoe with a day-old beard and an affinity for cheap scotch.

Much to her surprise, the ex–Navy SEAL and spy was a clean-cut, wiry five ten, with a full head of silver-white hair, who could have passed for a mild-mannered CPA.

"Thanks for coming in," Robin said as she approached Breland in the firm's waiting room.

"I appreciate the chance to interview," Breland said with a pleasant smile.

"Do you want some coffee or tea?"

"No, thanks."

"Then let's go back to my office."

"You have an impressive résumé," Robin said when they were seated. "I imagine you have more than a few war stories you could tell if you could convince the government to declassify your files."

Breland laughed. "There are one or two that might make a decent TV episode, but an account of most of my exploits would put you to sleep."

"I understand that Carrie Anders told you about this job."

Breland stopped smiling. "She did, and I'm sorry that there's an opening. I lost my wife to cancer, so I know how much pain you're experiencing."

Robin nodded, unable to speak for a moment because her heart had seized up. Eager to change the subject, she asked, "How much experience as an investigator do you have?"

"I was a policeman before I enlisted in the navy. After my time in the SEALs, I was a field agent in the Central Intelligence Agency, so I did my fair share of investigation before I retired."

"Mark told me that you volunteered to work cold cases."

"I did."

"Any results?"

"A few. Unfortunately, the arrests came too late to

save some people who would be alive if the responsible parties were arrested before the cases went cold."

"Mark said that he went over the salary, health insurance, and all the other employment stuff when you two talked."

Breland nodded.

"Well, we'd love to have you work as the firm's investigator if you're still interested."

"I am."

"When can you start?"

"Anytime you need me."

"Then consider yourself hired." Robin took something off the top of the pile of discovery in Marjorie's case before standing up. "Why don't I show you your office. Then I have a murder case I want you to work on."

"Sounds interesting."

"Unfortunately, it is," Robin said as they walked down the hall to the office that used to belong to Jeff. "I much prefer the uninteresting ones, especially if the evidence is in our favor."

Robin took a deep breath before ushering Breland into his new office. Breland walked around what used to be Jeff's desk and sat down. Robin sat across from him in the chair she'd sat in so often when she and Jeff talked about cases or just talked. "These are your new digs. When we're finished, I'll have Sally Yeats, our receptionist, come in and explain the phones, how to print to our copier, and all the other stuff you'll need to know."

"Tell me about the murder case," Breland said.

"Marjorie Loman is accused of torturing and killing her husband, but she may be innocent, and two men may have killed Joel Loman."

Breland nodded. "Who are these men?"

"That's what I need you to find out. We don't have names, but we're certain that they work for some enterprise in Oregon. They told Marjorie that her husband owed them a quarter of a million dollars, and she had to make good on the debt now that he was dead."

"So, loan sharks or something to do with gambling," Breland said.

"That's my guess."

Robin handed Breland the picture that Marjorie had taken with her phone. It showed two men standing outside of her apartment in Elk Grove.

"Marjorie says that these are the men who threatened her."

"This will be a big help. I still have contacts at the agency who owe me favors, and I have friends in the police. Someone should be able to get me the men's names and a lot more. Now, why don't you tell me everything I need to know to investigate this case."

Breland listened carefully as Robin brought him up to speed. When she finished, he was quiet for a while, and Robin let him think.

"If our client is innocent, we have two alternative theories to put in front of a jury—the two leg-breakers and Joel's partner."

Robin nodded.

"Do you know where we can find Kelly Starrett?" Breland asked. "I'd like to size her up."

CHAPTER THIRTY-SEVEN

Robin didn't have any trouble locating Kelly Starrett. An internet search told her that Starrett was a partner in Gold Coast Investments and that she was married to Nicholas Marques, the firm's founder. Moments after the receptionist told Starrett who wanted to see her, she and Ken were escorted to a large corner office with a view of the river and mountains.

Starrett was dressed in a business suit Robin knew had been created by a famous designer and cost a fortune. It looked like Joel's ex-partner had done quite well since the collapse of her firm.

"So, you're representing the bitch who murdered Joel," Starrett said when Robin and Ken were seated across from her.

"I represent Mrs. Loman."

Starrett grinned. "Marjorie is a bitch, but I bear her no ill will. In fact, I'm very grateful to her for getting rid of her piece-of-shit husband."

"Why is that?"

"You probably know that Joel embezzled millions from our firm. When Marjorie took off, I was in bad shape. I knew Nick, my husband, because we were in the same business. What I didn't know was that he wanted to date me, but stayed away because of Joel. Nick bailed out Emerald, we transferred Emerald's clients to Gold Coast, and then we married."

Starrett waved her hand across the office. "If Marjorie hadn't cleared the deck by getting rid of Joel, none of this would have been possible."

"Marjorie thinks you might have swabbed the deck," Robin said.

Starrett laughed. "Of course she does. But why would I kill Joel when I didn't know he'd robbed the firm until after he was dead?"

"You could have known before and pretended to be surprised."

"Is that what you're going to argue at Marjorie's trial to create a reasonable doubt?"

"Maybe."

Starrett shrugged. "Good luck. Obviously, the police never saw me as a serious suspect, but take your best shot."

"Did you ever recover the money Joel embezzled?"

Starrett's smile disappeared. "No. That's one of life's great mysteries. Believe me, if I knew where he'd hidden our clients' money, I'd have gotten it by now."

Robin stood. "Congratulations on your success. If you didn't kill Joel to get it, then my congratulations are heartfelt."

"What do you think?" Robin asked Ken when they were back on the street.

"I think Kelly Starrett is a very cool customer."

"She could also be a very good actress."

CHAPTER THIRTY-EIGHT

Two days later, Ken Breland rapped his fist on Robin's doorjamb. "Do you have a minute?"

Robin motioned Breland in.

"I know the identity of the two men who threatened our client," he said. "We're looking for Louis DeBello and Martin Callahan. They both have rap sheets overflowing with violent crimes."

"Do you know where we can find them?"

"They work at the Rainbow's End Casino for Cornell Stamoran."

"Doing what?"

"From what our client says, I'm guessing they're debt collectors."

The Rainbow's End Casino was the only Oregon

casino that was not on tribal land. The granting of the permit to operate had been very controversial because of Stamoran's reputation, and it had generated litigation and rumors of payoffs.

"Do you think we'll find them at the casino?" she asked Ken.

"I have no idea, but they're professional criminals. They won't talk to us."

Robin smiled like a person with a secret. "That might not be important."

Ken looked puzzled. "What's got you so excited?"

"An idea, but I want to run it by you, Mark, and Loretta to see if you all think I'm crazy."

After her meeting with Ken Breland, Robin drafted a memo that set out the facts in Marjorie Loman's Elk Grove and Portland cases and her theory of defense and gave it to Mark, Ken, and Loretta Washington.

Robin had nicknamed Loretta, a five-foot-one African American dynamo, the *Flash,* because she was always in motion. She'd grown up on the East Coast, and, like Robin, she was the first person in her family to go to college. A full ride at Lewis & Clark Law School had enticed her to Portland, where she'd finished high enough in her class to land a prestigious clerkship on the Oregon Supreme Court. Robin treasured Loretta's research skills, and she was also turning into an excellent trial attorney.

The next day, Robin convened a war council in the firm's conference room. Mark Berman was already there when Robin walked in. He was sipping Earl Grey tea as he read through the memo for the third time. Ken came in carrying a latte and his case file. When Loretta walked in, Robin told her to shut the conference room door.

"Have you all gotten a chance to read my memo?" Robin asked. Everyone nodded.

"What do you think about the strategy I'm contemplating?"

"You want to try this out at Loman's bail hearing?" Mark asked.

"It's set for next week," Robin answered.

"I don't know," Mark said. "It's awfully risky."

"I agree," Robin said, "but Vanessa will have an ethical duty to dismiss Marjorie's case if she has a reasonable doubt after reviewing the facts or actually be lieves that Marjorie is innocent."

"Vanessa is a career prosecutor," Mark countered. "She's going to let a jury decide Marjorie's fate unless you get DeBello or Callahan to confess on the stand, which they won't do unless you can convince Perry Mason to sit second chair."

Robin smiled. "It's the tactics that Perry uses in some of Gardner's books that gave me the idea."

Mark looked concerned. "You know those books and the TV show are scripted, so everything always comes out the way the writer wants it to? Marjorie's case isn't being tried on a television show."

"That's why we're having this brainstorming session. I want your honest opinion on my strategy at the bail hearing. If I guess wrong, I'll be giving a lot of ammunition to Vanessa."

When everyone had given their opinion, there was still no consensus. Ken and Loretta thought it was worth a gamble, but Mark thought Robin was making a mistake.

"What are you going to do?" Mark asked.

"I'm going to take the first step. There will still be plenty of opportunities to abort. Ken, get me some subpoenas."

CHAPTER THIRTY-NINE

Shortly after leaving Portland and its suburbs, Robin entered a picturesque landscape where low forested hills bordered fields of lush green crops, rich black soil, and yellow mown hay. Interspersed between the farms were vineyards, orchards, and small towns.

When the farmland disappeared, the two-lane highway wound through towering evergreen forests, where white water rushed over boulders within view of the road and patches of snow were visible even at the onset of summer.

After they crossed over the low mountains of the Coast Range, Robin turned south onto the highway that bordered the Pacific Ocean. To the west, violent waves crashed against massive rock formations before grinding to a halt on beaches that stretched beneath cliffs that had been eroded by centuries of wind and rain.

The Rainbow's End Casino was located just off the highway in one of the bigger towns on the coast. The casino and its three-story hotel sat in the middle of a vast parking lot that was crowded with cars.

Robin was dressed in a navy-blue blazer and a white, man-tailored shirt. Her .38 was tucked into a holster that was attached to her navy-blue slacks. Ken was wearing a windbreaker over jeans and a blue work shirt.

"I'm always amazed that people go to casinos on a day as beautiful as this," Robin said as they walked toward the entrance.

"I'm amazed that anyone gambles at all," Ken said. "Any fool knows that the odds always favor the house."

"Aah, but those odds are irrelevant if you're lucky."

The attorney and her investigator left sunny blue skies filled with white, puffy clouds and entered a dark world of flashing lights, ringing bells, moans, and excited shouts. Older people who didn't look like they could afford to lose fed quarters into one-armed bandits. Other bettors surrounded the roulette and craps tables or sat opposite a blackjack dealer and prayed for the cards that would make their fortune.

"How do you want to play this?" Ken asked.

"Why don't we split up and ask some of the staff if

they know where we can find DeBello and Callahan. If that doesn't work, we can go to Stamoran's office."

"Okay."

"Keep your phone on," Robin said. "I'll text you if I find them, and you do the same."

Ken disappeared into the crowd, and Robin spotted a waitress who had just handed a drink to a player at one of the blackjack tables.

"Hi, I wonder if you can help me?" Robin asked, flashing a breezy smile.

"Sure," the waitress answered, returning the smile the way she'd been instructed to by management.

"I'm looking for Lou DeBello and Martin Callahan. I was supposed to meet them on the floor, but I have no idea where to look."

The waitress seemed puzzled. "The names don't ring a bell. Do they work here?"

"That's what Lou said."

The waitress thought for a moment before shaking her head. "Sorry, I can't help you."

Robin got the same response from several other employees. She texted Ken, who'd had no more luck than Robin. They decided to go to Cornell Stamoran's office. Robin told Stamoran's secretary that she'd like to talk to him about DeBello and Callahan, but the secretary said that her boss wasn't in. Robin gave her a business card and asked her to have Stamoran call her.

"This looks like a dead end," Robin said.

"I'm thinking that the two gentlemen aren't on the regular payroll."

"That makes sense. If they're breaking legs for management, they probably get paid in cash and don't have health insurance or deductions for social security."

It was nice to be out in the fresh air again, and Robin blamed the nearby white noise of the surf and the gentle sea breeze for not noticing the two men who were approaching from the front and rear as she and Ken walked down a narrow row between the parked cars. Ken heard footsteps approaching and turned to face Lou DeBello, who towered over him.

"I hear you been looking for us," said a man with bright red hair who stepped in front of Robin.

"We have, Mr. Callahan," Robin answered. "We have a few questions we'd like to ask about your relationship with Joel and Marjorie Loman."

"We don't answer questions," Callahan said. "So, you and your friend should never bother us again."

"I'm Mrs. Loman's lawyer. It's my job to bother you."

"That's your problem," Callahan said.

"There's a bail hearing on Monday in Mrs. Loman's case," Ken told DeBello. "We have subpoenas for you. When you're in front of a judge, you'll have to answer our questions."

DeBello grabbed Ken by the front of his shirt. "You got wax in your ears? No questions, no subpoenas."

"Could you please let me go?" Ken asked.

"Listen, you dumb—"

DeBello stopped in midsentence because Ken had shaped the fingers of his right hand into a rigid spear and snapped the tip into DeBello's throat with the speed of a rattlesnake strike. DeBello's eyes went wide, his hands flew to his throat, and he fell to his knees.

Callahan froze, and Robin took advantage of the situation to pull out her .38.

"Lou is going to have trouble talking," Ken said, "so ask Martin your questions."

Callahan's eyes were fixed on Robin's gun. She smiled. "To answer your unspoken question, Martin, I have shot people, and I'll have no problem shooting you if you do something stupid. So, did you kill Joel Loman?"

"Fuck you."

"We weren't kidding about the subpoena," Robin said. "Can you do the honors, Ken?"

The investigator took two subpoenas out of his jacket pocket.

"There's a bail hearing on Monday. Be there," Robin said.

"Ever hear of the constitutionally guaranteed right to remain silent?" Callahan asked. "You can serve all the subpoenas you want, but we know our rights."

"We're dealing with a jailhouse lawyer, Robin, so I don't think we're going to get anywhere." He slipped one of the subpoenas into DeBello's jacket before holding out the other one to Callahan, who made no move to take it. Ken smiled and stuffed it in the redhead's pocket.

"See you in court," Robin said.

"You'll see our lawyers, bitch."

Robin smiled as she edged around Callahan and walked backward to her car, so she could keep the men in sight.

CHAPTER FORTY

The Multnomah County Courthouse is a building of stark gray concrete whose ominous exterior sends a clear message to those who enter that justice will be served without mercy to those who break the law. Inmates of the county jail who have a court appearance across the park are transported to a holding area on the seventh floor, and that is where Robin met with Marjorie Loman an hour before they were due in court.

"There's going to be a hearing this afternoon," Robin said. "I'm going to try to get you bail so you can get out of jail until the trial. I also want to try something else. If I'm successful, I may be able to have your murder case dismissed, but it's very risky, and I want to discuss the pros and cons with you so you can decide if you want me to try it."

"Go ahead," Marjorie said.

Robin explained what she wanted to do. Marjorie listened carefully, interrupting to ask questions.

"Here's where it could get tricky," Robin said. "I might have to call you to testify, which means that the DA can cross-examine you. What you say will be on the record and under oath and can be used against you at trial. So, you can see the potential problems."

Marjorie leaned forward, her eyes on her attorney and her lips set in a grim line. "I'm completely innocent, Robin. I did not kill Joel. Put me on the stand. I'm not afraid."

The Honorable Nanette LaBerge had been assigned to hear Marjorie's case. The judge, a former public defender, was a large woman with a big smile and an easygoing judicial temperament. Her former profession led attorneys to believe that she would favor the defense, but Judge LaBerge had spent her career doing lunch with criminals, most of whom were guilty, so she had no illusions about them. Those defense attorneys who assumed that they had a friend on the bench learned very quickly that they would get no breaks in Nanette's court.

The stately courtroom where the bail hearing was going to be held was the exact opposite of the courtroom in Elk Grove where Marjorie had faced charges of kidnapping and assault. It had a high ceiling decorated with ornate molding, marble Corinthian columns, and a polished wood dais. The uncomfortable wooden benches in the spectator section were the only thing the courtrooms had in common.

As Robin walked down the aisle toward the bar of the court, she spotted Lou DeBello and Martin Callahan sitting with two well-known criminal defense attorneys. Loretta Washington followed Robin and took a seat in the spectator section behind her. Ken Breland sat in the last row.

As soon as Robin was seated at the defense counsel table, the guards led Marjorie to her. Loretta had brought a conservative gray suit and a white blouse to the jail so Marjorie looked like a businesswoman instead of a dangerous inmate. Moments after her client was seated beside Robin, the judge took the bench.

"Good afternoon, Miss Lockwood and Mrs. Cole. I understand the defense is requesting bail for Mrs. Loman."

"That's right, Your Honor," Robin said.

"This being a murder case, I have to deny bail if Mrs. Cole can convince me that the proof is evident or the presumption is strong that Mrs. Loman is guilty. So, Mrs. Cole, what do you have to say about your case?"

"Roger Dillon, one of the homicide detectives who is working this case, will summarize our evidence."

"Detective," Vanessa said as soon as Dillon was sworn, "can you please tell the judge what proof we can produce that will prove that Mrs. Loman murdered her husband?"

Roger turned to face Judge LaBerge. "The defendant was married to Joel Loman, whose body was found behind a Portland restaurant. He'd been tortured, then shot. The Lomans were going through an acrimonious divorce. Prior to filing, Joel Loman took all the money from the couple's bank accounts, converted it to gold, and hid it from the defendant. During the course of our investigation, we discovered that no one knew where the gold was being held. One possible motive for torturing Mr. Loman would be to discover the location of the gold.

"After Mr. Loman's body was discovered, my partner, Carrie Anders, and I drove to Profit, Oregon, where the couple had their home. When we told the defendant that her husband was dead, she laughed and said that was great news. She also made several disparaging remarks about the deceased.

"A few days after Mr. Loman's body was discovered, we returned to the Lomans' house to ask her more questions. The house was deserted. The defendant is a police officer on the Profit, Oregon, police force. We contacted her supervisor, who told us that she had not been to work for several days. Shortly after that, a Mercedes car that the victim leased for his business was discovered in a parking lot at the airport.

"Detective Anders and I secured a search warrant for the car and home, and a forensic team discovered blood that was subsequently identified as Joel Loman's in the entryway of the home and his blood and hair in the car trunk. DNA from the defendant was also found in the trunk of the car.

"A year after Mrs. Loman disappeared, we learned that she was being tried in a town in the Midwest named Elk Grove for kidnapping a child and assaulting the child and her mother. Mrs. Loman had been calling herself Ruth Larson, and she had forged identification in that name. We went to Elk Grove and arrested her on the charge of murdering her husband."

"That's what the evidence in our case will show, Your Honor," Vanessa said.

"Miss Lockwood," the judge said.

"Thank you. Detective Dillon, did you sit through Mrs. Loman's trial in Elk Grove?"

"I did."

"Wasn't Mrs. Loman acquitted of all the charges at that trial?"

"Yes."

"Detective, has Mrs. Loman ever confessed to killing her husband?"

"No."

"In fact, she has consistently denied killing him, hasn't she?"

"Yes."

"You told the judge that Mrs. Loman laughed and made disparaging remarks about her husband after being told that he was dead."

"Yes."

"Isn't it true that after her initial reaction, she told you that she and Joel had been high school sweethearts who had married young and had grown apart because he was into drugs, drinking, and partying and she wanted to get away from that lifestyle?"

"Yes."

"After her initial reaction, didn't she seem sad that the marriage had disintegrated?"

"Her attitude did change."

"During her trial in Elk Grove, did you learn that Mrs. Loman claimed that two men had come to her home in Profit, Oregon, shortly after you told her that her husband had been tortured and murdered?"

"Yes."

"Did you learn that Mrs. Loman claimed that these men had implied that they had killed Joel and demanded that she pay them a quarter of a million dollars he owed as a gambling debt?"

"That's what she claimed."

"Didn't she say that she ran away from Oregon and hid out because she was in fear of her life?"

"That was her story."

"Didn't she also claim that the two men had shown up in Elk Grove?"

"That's what she claimed."

"Did Mrs. Loman have her service revolver with her when she was arrested on the Elk Grove charges?"

"Yes."

"Isn't it true that Mrs. Loman's gun did not fire the bullet that killed Mr. Loman?"

"Yes."

"Was Mr. Loman a partner in a firm that invested money for clients?"

"Yes."

"Was his partner named Kelly Starrett?"

"Yes."

"Have you learned that Mr. Loman embezzled millions of dollars from his firm and hid it?"

"Yes."

"Miss Starrett would have a motive to murder Mr. Loman, wouldn't she?"

"I guess."

"And the car you found at the airport was a company car, not a car registered to the home in which Mrs. Loman lived?"

"Yes."

"Was it usually parked in the building where the investment firm did business?"

"Yes."

"Was DNA and hair that matched Miss Starrett also found in the Mercedes?"

"Yes."

"Nothing further, Your Honor," Robin said.

"Do you have any more witnesses, Mrs. Cole?" the judge asked.

In a bail hearing, the prosecution usually called one investigator to outline their case so the defense did not get a chance to cross-examine her other witnesses.

"We rest," Vanessa said.

"Miss Lockwood?" the judge asked.

"Mrs. Loman calls Kenneth Breland."

"Mr. Breland, how are you employed?" Robin asked after Breland was sworn in.

"I'm an investigator in your firm."

"Did Mrs. Loman give you her cell phone?"

"Yes."

"Was there a picture on the phone of two men outside the apartment in Elk Grove where she was living?"

"Yes."

"Were you able to confirm that Mrs. Loman stayed in this apartment?"

"Yes."

"I'd like an enlargement of the photograph taken by the cell phone admitted as Defense Exhibit 1."

"Any objection, Mrs. Cole?" the judge asked.

"For purposes of this hearing, I don't have one," answered Vanessa, who wanted to see as much of the defense evidence as she could.

"Mr. Breland," Robin asked, "were you able to determine the identity of the men in the photograph?"

"Yes."

"Who are they?"

"Louis DeBello and Martin Callahan."

"Are Mr. DeBello and Mr. Callahan in the courtroom?"

"Yes."

"Can you point them out for Judge LaBerge?"

"They're the two large gentlemen seated in the back of the courtroom," Ken said.

"Do Mr. Callahan and Mr. DeBello have lengthy criminal records, including arrests and convictions for crimes of violence?"

"Yes."

"I'd like the rap sheets of Mr. DeBello and Mr. Callahan entered as Defense Exhibits 2 and 3."

"No objection," Vanessa said.

"Did you determine where they worked?"

"Yes. They are employees of the Rainbow's End Casino."

"Is that located here in Oregon?"

"Yes."

"No further questions, Your Honor."

"Mrs. Cole?"

"No cross, Your Honor."

"Mrs. Loman calls Louis DeBello," Robin said.

DeBello glared at Robin and Marjorie as he walked to the witness stand and was sworn.

"Mr. DeBello, are you employed by the Rainbow's End Casino in Oregon?"

"On advice of counsel, I decline to answer on the grounds that my answer may tend to incriminate me."

Robin wanted to give a fist pump, but she restrained herself. She had hoped that DeBello and Callahan would refuse to answer her questions, and her gamble was paying off.

"Mr. DeBello, on the day after Joel Loman's dead and tortured body was discovered, did you and Martin Callahan drive to Marjorie Loman's home in Profit, Oregon?"

"On advice of counsel, I decline to answer on the grounds that my answer may tend to incriminate me."

"Did you tell Mrs. Loman that her husband owed a quarter of a million dollars and that she was responsible for the debt now that Mr. Loman was dead?"

DeBello repeated his assertion of his right to remain silent.

"Did you imply that you had murdered Mr. Loman?"

DeBello pled the Fifth.

"Isn't it true that you and Martin Callahan murdered Joel Loman and placed his dead body in Mrs. Loman's house to terrify her into paying Joel's debt."

"I refuse to answer on the grounds that my answer may tend to incriminate me."

"Did you go to Elk Grove looking for Mrs. Loman approximately a year after Mr. Loman was murdered?"

DeBello pled the Fifth.

"No further questions, Your Honor."

Vanessa waived cross. When he left the witness stand, DeBello focused his anger on Marjorie.

Robin called Martin Callahan, who refused to answer the same questions Robin had asked DeBello. When Robin excused Callahan, he walked up the aisle, and one of the men who had been sitting next to him and DeBello walked to the bar of the court.

"Your Honor, my name is Thomas Coyne."

"I recognize you, Mr. Coyne."

The lawyer smiled. "I represent Mr. Callahan, and Michael First represents Mr. DeBello. We'd like to know if their attendance is required any longer."

"Miss Lockwood, are you through with these witnesses?" the judge asked.

"I don't intend to call them again. Unless Mrs. Cole wants them here, they can leave."

"Mrs. Cole?" the judge asked.

"No, Your Honor."

"They can go."

"Thank you," Coyne said.

As DeBello passed Ken Breland, he said, "This isn't over." Breland didn't react.

"Do you have any more witnesses, Miss Lockwood?"

"One, Your Honor. Marjorie Loman wants to tell you what happened."

Vanessa looked shocked when Marjorie walked to the witness stand. Judge LaBerge frowned. If Robin were a new attorney, the judge would have called a sidebar and asked her if she was insane, but Robin had an exemplary reputation, and the judge decided that Robin had something up her sleeve if she was going to risk a cross-examination under oath by one of the most highly skilled prosecutors in the state.

"Mrs. Loman," Robin said, "please tell the judge when you first discovered that your husband had been murdered."

Marjorie took a sip of water. Then she turned to the judge. "I found Joel's body the night before Detectives Anders and Dillon came to my house."

It took all Vanessa's self-control to keep her jaw from dropping.

"I was working as a deputy sheriff in the Profit Police Department. I came home from my shift, and Joel was in the entryway. It was obvious that he had been killed and tortured."

"Why did you think the body had been left in your entryway?"

"Joel had been involved with drugs, gambling, and other vices that brought him in contact with dangerous people. That was one reason why we had grown apart. I didn't want that lifestyle anymore. It was common knowledge that we were going through a really bad divorce. My initial thought when I found Joel was that his body had been left in my house to frame me, because I had a motive to kill him."

"Why didn't you report the murder to the police?" Robin asked.

"I was stupid. I know that now. I should have reported the crime, but I thought that the killer had probably tipped off the police to frame me, and I panicked because I thought the police might show up any minute."

"What did you do?"

"The Mercedes that Joel leased for his business was parked in front of our house. I put the body in the trunk of the car. Then I drove it to Portland and left Joel in an alley behind a restaurant."

"Did the police come to your house?"

"No, but those two men did come the next day and threatened me."

"Were the men you just referred to in the courtroom today?" Robin asked.

"Yes. They just testified."

"We're talking about Louis DeBello and Martin Callahan?"

"Yes."

"Okay. Now, you just told the judge that Mr. DeBello and Mr. Callahan came to your home in Profit. What did they say to you?"

"They said what happened to Joel would happen to me if I didn't pay them two hundred fifty thousand dollars. That's why I ran. Joel had gutted our accounts and hidden our assets. All I had was my salary from the police department. Since I wouldn't be able to pay the men a quarter of a million dollars, I was sure I'd be killed. That's why I ran to Elk Grove. I thought I'd be safe there, but those men showed up looking for me, and I ran again. And that's the truth. I never killed Joel. I hated him, but I never wanted him to die that way. It was horrible what they did to him."

Marjorie choked up and stopped talking. Robin waited until Marjorie regained her composure.

"Do you know a woman named Kelly Starrett?"

"Yes."

"Was she your husband's partner in his investment firm?"

"Yes."

"Was your husband having an affair with Miss Starrett?"

"Yes."

"Have you learned that Joel embezzled a large amount of money from the firm?"

"Yes."

"Your witness," Robin told Vanessa.

Vanessa looked like a lion that had just been thrown a slab of bloody meat.

"You hated your husband, didn't you?"

"Yes."

"And you laughed when the detectives told you he was dead."

"Everyone knew how vicious the divorce was. Looking sad would make me look suspicious."

"You tried to get rid of the blood in your entryway and the trunk of the Mercedes to cover up your crime, didn't you?"

"I did my best to get rid of evidence that Joel's body had been inside the house and the car trunk, but I didn't do that because I'd killed him. I did it because I was being framed."

"You were a police officer. You could have reported the murder instead of dumping your husband's body."

"Getting rid of Joel's body was incredibly stupid, but I was terrified. I probably should have called 911 when I found him. As a police officer, I've seen dead bodies, but I've never seen the body of someone I knew and once cared for. And . . ." Marjorie paused and took a breath. "He'd been mutilated." She shook her head. "I was in shock, and I wasn't thinking straight."

"After you'd had some time to think, you still didn't go to the authorities, did you? You went on the run."

Marjorie looked Vanessa in the eye. "Mrs. Cole, once I got rid of my husband's body, I realized that I looked incredibly guilty, and I believed that I had three choices. I could stay in Oregon and be tortured and killed by DeBello and Callahan, I could stay and be charged with a murder I didn't commit, or I could run. Maybe I should have stuck around, but I saw hiding as the only way to stay out of a jail cell or a grave."

"You want Judge LaBerge to believe that you aren't a violent person, don't you?"

"I did not kill Joel."

"But, in Elk Grove, you did kidnap a baby and abuse that child and pistol-whip the baby's mother, didn't you?"

"I never abused my little boy. A jury was convinced I could never hurt my baby and acquitted me. The jurors also understood that I was mentally ill when I took the Lindstroms' child and hit Emily. I feel terrible about hurting her. But I never would have done any of that if those men hadn't shown up in Elk Grove. When I saw them, it pushed me over the edge."

Vanessa continued to question Marjorie, but she answered every question with such conviction that

Robin was sure that she had made the right choice when she put her on the stand. Finally, a frustrated Vanessa stopped her cross-examination, and Marjorie's ordeal ended.

"Mrs. Loman has no more witnesses," Robin said.

"Mrs. Cole?" the judge asked.

"None, Your Honor."

"Do you want to argue about the bail, Mrs. Cole, because I have to tell you that I am inclined to grant it."

Vanessa looked upset. "The defendant hated her husband, there's proof he was killed in her house, she laughed when she was told he was dead, she admitted that she got rid of his body, and she ran. That's more than enough proof to convince a jury that Mrs. Loman is guilty."

"What about DeBello and Callahan?"

"They didn't admit they murdered Joel Loman."

"They sure didn't deny it," the judge answered. "In fact, they looked guilty as hell. And there is proof that they followed Mrs. Loman to Elk Grove. Then there's some evidence of another person who had a motive to kill Mr. Loman. Miss Starrett's DNA was found in the Mercedes, and he embezzled money from their firm and ruined it. No, Mrs. Cole, after what I've just heard, I can't say that the proof is evident or the presumption is strong that Mrs. Loman is guilty. I'd say that you can make as good a case against those two hoods as you can against Mrs. Loman. So, I'm going to set bail.

Let's go in chambers and hash out the amount and conditions."

When she returned to the courtroom, Robin told Marjorie how much money she would have to post for bail to get out of jail.

"You'll also have to surrender your passport and agree to stay in Oregon."

"That's not a problem. How long until I'm out of jail?"

"A few hours. I'll have my associate work with you on getting the bail posted. Do you have a place to stay?"

"I hadn't thought about that."

"I have a friend with rental property. There's a house in the country she'll let you stay at. It's on a wooded lot and very quiet. I thought you might enjoy a little peace after spending so much time in jail."

"Thank you, Robin. You're amazing."

"No, I'm relieved. You do realize that I played dice with your life."

"With you at the table, the dice were loaded," Marjorie said.

"How are you feeling?" Robin asked when Marjorie walked out of the elevator in the jail reception area.

"Like I can use a shower and a decent meal."

"I had one of my associates stock the refrigerator at the house you'll be staying at. You can shower and chow down after I drop you off."

"I don't know how to thank you for everything you've done."

"Wait until you're free and clear before heaping on the praise. My car's a block away."

Marjorie was quiet during the walk to Robin's garage, and she spent the drive wrapped up in her own thoughts. Robin appreciated the silence because a heavy rain started falling as soon as they pulled out of the lot, and Robin had to concentrate, especially when they turned off the highway onto a narrow, two-lane country road.

When Robin left the garage, she thought she saw a car following her, but she chalked up the thought to an overactive imagination. During the trip along the highway, she thought she saw the car again, but the rain was very heavy, and she couldn't be certain. During the final stretch of their trip, Robin looked in her rearview mirror once or twice, but she didn't see anyone behind her.

The two-story ranch house where Marjorie was staying backed on thick woods. The closest neighbor was a quarter of a mile away. A long driveway led up to the garage. Robin parked in front of the house and was running for the shelter of the overhang that shielded the front door when she heard a car approaching from the direction of the highway. She turned just as the car drove by the driveway and kept going. It could have been the car she thought might be tailing her, but she couldn't be certain.

CHAPTER FORTY-ONE

Two days after the bail hearing, Robin was dragged out of a deep sleep when the ringtone on her phone played the opening chords of "Rockin' Robin," the music that played during her ring walk when she fought in UFC events. Robin groped for her phone and sat up. The clock on her end table said it was twenty after three.

"They're here," Marjorie said in a terrified whisper.

"What?"

"DeBello and Callahan. I . . . I shot them. They're dead. What should I do?"

Robin was wide awake now. "Don't do anything until I get there. I'm on the way."

Rain pounded Robin's windshield, making it hard to see during the drive. Robin passed a black sedan that was parked by the side of the road, out of sight of the house, but she didn't see any other cars when she turned up the driveway. All the lights were on in the house when Robin parked. She drew her gun and crept toward the front door. The shades were up in a window on the living room side of the door, and Robin saw Marjorie slumped on a sofa.

The front door was ajar, and gusts of wind blew rain into the entryway.

"Marjorie, it's Robin. Is it safe to come in?"

"I killed them."

Robin walked inside and stopped. Callahan sprawled on his back inches from Robin's feet. Several bullet holes were spaced across his chest, and a gun lay within inches of his outstretched hand. DeBello was lying facedown in a pool of blood on the bottom steps of the stairs that led up to the second floor.

Marjorie was wearing flannel pajamas, and her face was drained of color. As Robin walked into the living room, she saw a .45 Magnum lying on the sofa. She stopped in front of Marjorie. "What happened?"

"They got inside. I went to the top of the stairs and asked them what they wanted. DeBello said Joel had died before he could talk, but they'd keep me alive until I told them where the gold was hidden and how to get it. They said I had to tell them where Joel hid the gold or they'd kill me. So, I shot them."

"Where did you get the gun?"

"DeBello stared at me at the bail hearing. He looked so angry. I was afraid. I knew a man who sells guns. I knew it was illegal, but I got one for protection."

Robin took out her phone. "I'm going to call the police. Don't say anything when they get here. I'll do the talking."

"This is bullshit, Robin," Carrie Anders fumed. "Your client executed these men."

"Did you see the gun next to Callahan?" Robin asked. "And what were two leg-breakers doing inside Marjorie's house at three in the morning? Those men were after the gold. They admitted torturing Joel to find out where it was, and they threatened to torture Marjorie until she told them."

"So she says."

"Look, Carrie, Marjorie doesn't know where Joel hid the gold. She would have died because she didn't know. She had no choice. It was self-defense."

"At least we have her on a weapons violation," Carrie said.

"Jesus, Carrie. You're not that petty."

Carrie turned red with anger, but held her tongue.

"I'm going to sit with my client," Robin said, and she headed for the kitchen where a police officer was keeping an eye on Marjorie.

"What's going to happen now?" Marjorie asked.

"You're probably going back to jail until we can clear this up. But I think you'll be okay."

"What if the casino sends more men after me?"

"I'll talk to the owner, but I can't see that happening after this. I think Stamoran is going to forget Joel's debt or face serious charges."

Marjorie closed her eyes. "I don't want to go back."

Robin put a hand on her shoulder. "I know. Hang in there. I'll talk to Vanessa, and I'll get this in front of a judge as soon as I can."

CHAPTER FORTY-TWO

Vanessa had sent Robin the police reports of the investigation into the shooting at Marjorie's house. After reading them, Robin didn't think the State had the ammunition it would need to get an indictment, let alone a conviction for anything other than a weapons-possession charge. The judge at Marjorie's bail hearing had reached the same conclusion, and Marjorie was out on bail again.

A week after the bail hearing, Robin walked across town in a cold, sloppy rain to the restaurant where she had arranged to meet her client. The maître d' escorted Robin to the table where Marjorie was waiting.

"How have you been?" Robin asked as she slid into the seat across from her client.

"Pretty good, considering."

"Well, you're going to feel a whole lot better when I tell you why I wanted to meet. Vanessa dismissed your murder case, and she's not going to charge you in the shooting at the house or for possession of a weapon."

Marjorie looked like she didn't understand what Robin had just said. Robin smiled. "You don't have any charges against you. You'll get back your bail and your passport, and you're free to go anywhere you want."

"My God! So, it's over?"

"Not completely. Vanessa isn't convinced you're innocent, so she didn't dismiss with prejudice. If she had, she would be barred from prosecuting you for Joel's murder. If she finds new evidence, she could indict you again."

"Isn't there some kind of statute of limitations?"

"Not for murder. But you shouldn't worry. If they had the goods, Vanessa would have gone to trial."

"Why did she dismiss?" Marjorie asked.

"It was DeBello and Callahan. There's no way Vanessa could prove you weren't acting in self-defense when you shot them. And evidence about the home invasion would bolster our argument that they killed Joel while they were trying to find out where he hid the gold. It raised a reasonable doubt in her mind, and Vanessa is very, very ethical."

Marjorie closed her eyes and took a deep breath. "This is hard to believe. My life has been hell since I found Joel's body. I can't imagine what it will be like waking up in the morning without the threat of prison hanging over my head."

"I'm guessing that you'll adjust pretty quickly."

Marjorie signaled the waitress. "We have to celebrate. What's your favorite cocktail or wine, or we could get a bottle of champagne? And lunch is on me."

"I'll toast the end of your ordeal with hot coffee. I'm still freezing from the cold and rain."

When the waitress left with their order, Robin asked, "What will you do now?"

"I'll have to think about that. But one thing is certain. I'm not staying in Oregon. When can I get my passport and the money I posted for bail?"

"I'm already working on that. I'll call when everything is set."

Marjorie reached across the table and laid her hand on Robin's. "There aren't enough words to thank you, Robin."

"I'm just glad your ordeal is over."

CHAPTER FORTY-THREE

Three weeks after the case against Marjorie Loman was dismissed, Robin went to court at nine for a short appearance. The matter was over at nine fifteen, and her next appearance was at ten thirty. Rather than go back to her office, Robin headed for a coffee shop near the courthouse. When she was ordering, she saw Carrie Anders sitting at a table by herself. Robin carried her latte to Carrie's table.

"Can I join you?" Robin asked.

"You must be feeling pretty good about the Loman case," Carrie said as Robin sat down.

Robin shrugged. The last time Robin had talked to Marjorie, she said that she was going to Arizona.

"You know she killed Joel Loman, right?" Carrie said.

"Are you saying that because you have a gut feeling or because you have something concrete that makes you think Marjorie killed her spouse?"

"Did you ever wonder how Starrett or DeBello and Callahan got into Loman's house to leave the body?" Carrie asked.

"What do you mean?"

"Your client told me and Roger that she changed the locks to keep her hubby from stealing the furniture, so Joel didn't have a key. That means the killer had to force entry into the house. But we walked around the house, and we didn't see any signs of forced entry."

"That doesn't prove anything. DeBello and Callahan are professional criminals. They'd know how to break in without leaving a trace."

"Maybe, but here's something else to think about. Wouldn't Joel have used some of the money he'd stashed away to pay his debt to the casino? Why let himself be tortured and killed when a simple bank transfer would have gotten DeBello and Callahan off his back? If you add in the money Joel embezzled to the sum he took from his and Marjorie's joint accounts, the gold Joel hid would be worth north of ten million dollars. A quarter of a million wouldn't dent that."

"You make some good points, but the case is over as far as I'm concerned."

"It isn't for me," Carrie said. "If Marjorie screws up, I'll be waiting for her."

Her talk with Carrie had made Robin uneasy. When she was back in her office, she reread the police reports of the shooting at Marjorie's house. A list of DeBello's and Callahan's possessions was included in the discovery. She scanned it quickly and tossed it onto the pile of documents she'd finished reading.

After a while, Robin had a hard time concentrating, so she headed home at four. She wasn't much of a cook, but there were a few simple pasta dishes she did well. By the time she was starting to eat, the mountains were hidden behind heavy, dark clouds, and rain was falling on the river.

Robin thought about Marjorie Loman as she dug into her spaghetti carbonara. If Marjorie were innocent, she'd done a good thing by winning her case. But what if she were guilty? Robin decided that she would have voted not guilty if she'd been on Marjorie's jury, but would that have been because the State could not prove guilt beyond a reasonable doubt or because she believed that Marjorie was innocent of any wrongdoing? There was a big difference.

The points Carrie had made bothered Robin, as did the fact that Marjorie had concealed proof that DeBello and Callahan had followed her to Elk Grove because she'd figured out that it would help her insanity defense if Dr. Suarez and the jurors believed that the men were a figment of her imagination.

Robin also saw a problem with pegging Kelly Starrett as Joel's killer. If she murdered Joel and left his body in the entryway of Marjorie's house to frame Marjorie for the killing, wouldn't she have called the police to tell them about the body? But the police never showed up at Marjorie's house.

Had Marjorie conned everyone? Did that matter? Robin had done the job she'd been hired to do. DeBello and Callahan were dead. If they'd killed Joel, they'd taken their secret to the grave, and Starrett had no reason to confess if she were guilty. So, no one would ever know for sure who had murdered Joel Loman.

Robin went to bed and was almost asleep when she thought about the list detailing DeBello's and Callahan's property. A jolt of adrenaline coursed through her, and she shot up in bed. It wasn't something in the list that upset her. It was something that should have been listed but was not. Everything that had been found in the men's car and on their person had been cataloged. Robin was certain that neither man's cell phone was anywhere on the list.

Robin thought through the implications and broke into a sweat. Was Marjorie a cold-blooded killer? One line of reasoning ended with that conclusion. Robin got up and walked to the window in her living room. There were a few lights on in the apartments across the way. She stared at them without seeing them as her thoughts whirled around without coming to a complete stop.

If she were prosecuting Marjorie, the fact that neither man had a cell phone would not be enough to convene a grand jury. But it was tilting her off the fence she'd been riding whenever she tried to decide if Marjorie was guilty or innocent. Was there a way to find the truth? Probably not, unless . . .

PART SIX

GOLD

A YEAR AND A HALF LATER

CHAPTER FORTY-FOUR

Marjorie had never been on a tropical island, and she felt like she'd walked into the steam room at her gym when she stepped off the plane in St. Therese. It didn't get much better in the terminal, where the only air came through the louvers in the small, one-story structure. She took a cab to her resort and checked in under the name Stephanie Baxter, using the second set of false IDs she'd had prepared when she'd commissioned her Ruth Larson identification. The fake ID had worked as perfectly in the hotel as it had when she'd bought her airline ticket and gone through passport control.

Marjorie had stored the Baxter passport, credit card, and driver's license in a safe-deposit box in a bank in a small town she had passed through on her way to Elk

Grove, knowing that she wouldn't use it until enough time passed for the authorities to lose interest in Joel's murder.

After her case was dismissed, Marjorie had moved to Arizona and lain low for a while, living on the money left over from the sale of Joel's penthouse and her home. Then, when she thought she'd be safe, she'd collected the Stephanie Baxter IDs and booked a flight to paradise.

Marjorie was jet-lagged and exhausted from the long flight to the Caribbean. After a fruity cocktail and a light dinner, she crashed in her air-conditioned room. When she woke up, she was refreshed and spent the morning on the beach. After a light lunch, Marjorie showered, then changed into an outfit that made her look like a business executive before gathering the paperwork that proved that Joel was dead, and that she was his lawfully wedded wife.

A taxi took her to Old Town, which was the habitat of colorfully painted buildings that sold Patek Philippe, Tiffany, Armani, and other international badges of wealth. Marjorie got out in the center of town and window-shopped. When she was convinced that she had not been followed, she wandered out of the shopping district into an area a few blocks from the ocean populated by three-story buildings that contained small offices sporting grandiose names like the St. Therese International Bank of Commerce that were outfitted with little more than a desk, a filing cabinet, and a phone. These banks were havens for the offshore accounts of crooked hedge fund operators, drug lords, and scheming, despicable husbands like Joel Loman.

Marjorie walked down a side street until she came to a building whose stark modern architecture clashed with the cheery, multicolored island décor. An elegant black woman wearing a dark business suit was seated behind a desk in an air-conditioned reception area decorated with dark woods, a glass coffee table, and leather-upholstered sofas and armchairs.

"Welcome to the St. Therese Depository," she said in island-accented French. "How may I help you?"

"I have an appointment with Monsieur Henri Broussard," Marjorie answered in English.

The woman glanced at a calendar on her desk before responding in impeccable English. "Mrs. Loman?"

Marjorie nodded.

The woman flashed a warm smile. "May I see some identification?"

Marjorie presented her real passport and driver's license. When she finished studying Marjorie's documents, the woman stood. "Please follow me. Can I get you something to drink? Coffee, tea, champagne?"

"I'm fine, thank you."

The woman stopped in front of a door at the end of a short hall and opened it. Marjorie walked into a room decorated in a nautical theme. Model sailboats, yachts, and ocean liners stood on a low cabinet and on shelving, and photographs and oils depicting sailing vessels on the high seas hung on the walls.

A slender black man of medium height stood when Marjorie walked in. He was dressed in a white suit, yellow tie, and pale blue shirt, and he studied Marjorie through wire-rimmed glasses.

"It's a pleasure to meet you, Mrs. Loman," the man said as Marjorie's escort backed out of the office and shut the door. "How can I be of service?"

Marjorie took a seat across the desk from Henri Broussard and handed him a manila envelope. "I was married to Joel Loman, and we lived in Oregon. Joel passed away a couple of years ago."

"I'm sorry for your loss."

"Thank you. His death certificate is in the envelope along with our marriage license. Joel converted our assets to gold. When he died, no one knew where he had hidden our money, and it took some time to find out that you have been storing the gold. I'm entitled to the assets since I was married to Joel when he passed away.

"In the envelope is a letter from Joel's attorney and another from my attorney establishing my claim. Also in the envelope is a list of accounts in several banks. I would like the gold to be converted into currency and deposited in the amounts I've designated. I've included photocopies of all the documents, which you can keep."

Broussard emptied the contents of the envelope onto his desk and read each document slowly while Marjorie waited.

"I will have to verify your claim, but everything appears to be in order."

"How long will the verification process last?"

"Not long. A day or two. Are you staying on the island?"

"Yes."

Broussard smiled. "There are worse places to have to wait. Enjoy the sun and sea."

"Please contact me through my cell or email," Marjorie told Broussard to avoid questions that might have arisen if she'd given him the number of her resort where she was registered under an alias.

"Of course," Broussard said, "and I will try to get everything in order as quickly as possible." Broussard handed back the envelope with the originals of the documents. Moments later, Marjorie was back in the center of town eyeing a pair of diamond earrings, which she would soon be able to afford.

CHAPTER FORTY-FIVE

Henri Broussard was on the money when he told Marjorie that there were worse places to have to wait to be told that you were worth millions. Marjorie got a Thai massage in the resort spa in the morning. Then she ate lunch while sipping a piña colada and staring at an ocean so blue it didn't look real.

While she ate, Marjorie fantasized about everything she would do once she had her money. First and foremost, she would rescue Peter from Elk Grove. Her beautiful son was not going to grow up in some backwater like she had. She would take him to Europe and send him to the best private schools. He would have the best of everything.

Marjorie was in the middle of her fantasy when she saw someone she had hoped to never see again walking toward her with another person she didn't recognize.

"How's the drink, Miss Baxter?" Carrie Anders asked.

Marjorie kept her composure when the detective used her fake name. "It's delicious. The food is great too. I had a lobster to die for last night. Are you staying here?"

Carrie laughed. "On a government per diem? I wish. No. Our flight leaves at eight tonight, so, unfortunately I won't be here long enough to enjoy the lobster."

"Why are you here?"

"I'm here to arrest you for Joel Loman's murder."

"You think I killed Joel?"

"I know you did."

Marjorie flashed a tolerant smile. "Kelly Starrett or the two leg-breakers employed by the casino murdered Joel. There's no proof that I did anything to him."

"Actually, there is, and you supplied it by flying here to claim the gold."

"What are you talking about?"

"Why was Joel Loman tortured? The most logical answer is that the person who tortured him wanted to find where he'd hidden the gold. After he talked, only two people in the whole world knew where Joel hid his gold: Joel and the person who killed him.

"Once you learned where the gold was hidden, you realized you couldn't fly to St. Therese right away without incriminating yourself. When DeBello and Callahan came after you, you hid in Elk Grove. Being a surrogate was perfect. You didn't have a lot of money, and you couldn't use your credit cards, so you needed a job. The surrogacy paid well, and it takes nine months to have a baby. You knew you had to wait at least a year for everyone to stop looking for you.

"That presented us with a problem. How could we learn when you were going to reclaim the gold? That's when we thought about your fake ID. We asked the Profit police chief if you'd ever worked on the case of someone who made false IDs. Randy Barrett told us about the Stephanie Baxter passport, credit card, and driver's license. We put your name and Stephanie Baxter on a watch list. As soon as you bought your ticket for St. Therese, we knew where the gold was hidden. Unfortunately for you, St. Therese and the US of A have an extradition treaty."

Carrie turned to the man who had accompanied her. "This is Inspector Claude Durand of the St. Therese police. He's already talked to Henri Broussard. No transfers are going to be made until we sort out what you are entitled to and what belongs to the clients of your husband's old firm. Once we sort that out, I'm guessing that you'll still have enough in the commissary at the Oregon State Penitentiary to keep you in candy bars and soda pop for your entire life sentence."

Marjorie smiled. "Cute, but your case is entirely circumstantial. A good defense lawyer will blow it out of the water, and I'll have the very best when I hire Robin Lockwood to defend me."

CHAPTER FORTY-SIX

Robin's Wednesday started on a high note. During her morning workout at McGill's gym, she sparred with a young male MMA fighter and held her own. When she left the gym, the sun was shining, and she bought a latte, which she sipped on her way to her office. The great workout, the weather, and the warmth of her drink combined to create a sense of well-being, a feeling she was just beginning to experience again.

Robin was doing okay. Not great, but okay. The pain that had been unbearable for so long was now a dull ache, and there had been times when she was happy. That had been a problem for a while. Robin would get excited while she was watching a UFC event on TV or a movie. Then her good feelings would come to a screeching halt when she remembered that Jeff was dead, and she had no business being happy. But lately, she'd actually been happy without feeling guilty, which she hoped was a major turning point in her battle with depression and sorrow, her constant companions since Jeff had been stolen from her.

The publicity from winning Marjorie Loman's highly publicized murder case had brought Robin and the firm enough new business to warrant hiring a third associate, and Robin had notched a few significant victories following the dismissal of Marjorie's case, so business was good, and she was excited about her cases again.

Robin had decided that she would be open to seeing someone. She'd actually had a date with a doctor who had rowed crew with Mark at the University of Washington. Mark and his wife had made up a foursome, and the doctor had called the next day. She'd gone to a movie and dinner with him, but had backed out of a second date because she'd been too sad after the first. Still, it was a start.

"A Marjorie Loman called twice," the receptionist said when Robin walked into the law office.

"Did she leave a number?"

"She was calling from the jail."

Robin closed her office door and thought about Marjorie Loman as she sipped her latte. Did she want to meet with her ex-client? In the end, she decided that it would be cowardly not to.

* * *

Marjorie was waiting for Robin in a contact visiting room. She smiled when Robin walked in.

"We have to stop meeting like this," she said, repeating the joke Robin had made when they'd met at the Justice Center jail.

Robin thought Marjorie looked a little heavier than she'd been the last time she'd seen her, but she hadn't changed a lot otherwise.

"Thanks for coming. It looks like I'm going to need you again," Marjorie said.

"I'm not going to be able to help you this time."

"I can pay you a lot of money. I'm worth millions now that I have the money Joel stole from me."

"You need new blood working for you."

"Are you sure I can't tempt you? You can name your price."

"I'm going to give another lawyer a chance to become filthy rich," Robin said as she pushed a sheet of paper across the metal table. "A lawyer with fresh eyes will have a better chance of convincing a jury. I've written down a few names. They're all excellent."

"I'm innocent, Robin. I didn't kill Joel."

"We both know that's not true. You lied to me, Marjorie."

"Have you been talking to Mrs. Cole?"

"She told me you were arrested in St. Therese when you tried to get the gold."

"It's my gold."

"True, but you tortured your husband to find out where he put it, and then you killed him."

"I thought a client's guilt or innocence didn't matter to a defense attorney."

"It wouldn't matter if I were your defense attorney. But I'm also a human being, and torture makes me sick. So, I'm going to pass on being your lawyer, and I'm not going to wish you luck."

"How can you be so certain that I killed Joel?"

"How else would you know where the gold was hidden? And I'm pretty certain you murdered DeBello and Callahan."

"That's interesting. Why on earth would you think I wasn't defending myself?"

"The cell phones. Neither man had one on his person or in his car."

Marjorie frowned. "I'm not following you."

"DeBello's and Callahan's cell phone numbers are in Ken Breland's investigative report, which I gave you along with the other discovery. You got a burner phone when you got your gun. Then you called DeBello or Callahan and lured them to the house with a promise that you'd tell them where the gold was hidden. When they walked into your trap, you killed both of them. Then you took their phones and destroyed them and your burner so no one would know about the call that lured them to their death."

"My, my. You're a regular Sherlock Holmes, aren't you? Out of curiosity, have you found these phantom phones?"

"I haven't looked for them. That's a job for the police. But I'm guessing they were hidden in the house or on the grounds, but are long gone by now."

"Assuming that they ever existed. Tell me, have you shared your Sherlockian deduction with Vanessa Cole?"

"No."

Marjorie leaned toward Robin. She was still smiling when she said, "You'd be wise to keep this weird idea to yourself in case I'm the terrible person you think I am. Because I've beaten every case so far, and I'll have an excellent chance to beat this ridiculous murder charge. In which case, I'll be out and about with enough money to cause a lot of mischief."

Robin felt the temperature in the room drop, and a knot formed in her stomach. She stood up and rang for the guard. Moments later, the lock snapped and the door to the corridor opened.

"I'm not going to wish you good luck, Marjorie," Robin said before she left the contact visiting room. "I'm just going to hope that justice is served."

Robin didn't feel good when she left the jail. She had always prided herself on holding herself to the highest ethical standards, and she wasn't certain that she had not crossed a line.

Before Jeff was taken from her, Robin had held on to a view that most people were good, despite what she saw of the dark side of the universe every day in her criminal cases. When Jeff was killed, a black-and-white view of morality and ethics and a rosy view of the world around her vanished. Jeff's death had shifted Robin's world off its axis, and she had not felt grounded since he had disappeared from her life for no rational reason.

Marjorie Loman deserved to spend the rest of her life behind bars, but Robin knew she would probably have gotten away with torturing and killing her husband if Robin had not met Carrie Anders one evening in a country tavern where they had met on other occasions when they had traded information that had benefited both of them.

Robin thought that Marjorie was guilty when she won Marjorie's bail hearing, but she wasn't certain. She had eliminated the people working for the casino, because Joel would have used the hidden money to pay off his debt if he were tortured, but Kelly Starrett had a strong motive too.

Robin was certain that the person who tortured Joel did it to find out where he'd hidden the gold. Robin had formed an impression that Joel lacked the character to hold up under torture. If Joel had talked before he died, his killer knew where the gold was hidden, and that person would eventually go for it.

As soon as she came to that conclusion, Robin told Carrie an idea had occurred to her. Marjorie had a false ID in Elk Grove. If Carrie found the person who made the false ID, she could find out if he'd made IDs in another name. Then Carrie could wait until Marjorie used that false ID to make a trip to an offshore haven or follow Kelly Starrett if she made the trip.

Robin had been upset because Marjorie had played her from the beginning, but did that justify giving Carrie Anders a suggestion that had led to her former client's arrest? The case had been over when she did it. Marjorie had never told her about the forger, so she had not revealed a client's confidence. She had just been tired of being lied to and used.

Robin wished Jeff were with her. He would have known the right thing to say to ease her mind, but Jeff was gone and she was on her own, and she would have to live with the choice she'd made.

ACKNOWLEDGMENTS

I could not have written *The Darkest Place* without a lot of help from experts in several areas that were new to me. Lissa Kaufman explained how surrogacy works, Jan Alexander helped me craft the postpartum psychosis defense that Robin Lockwood uses so effectively in the book, and Dave Johnson taught me how to hide gold.

I am indebted to the Oregon Criminal Defense Lawyers Association for putting on the two-day seminar in 2019 that featured Martin Bertholf's discussion of the shaken baby syndrome and to Mark Brown, Janis Puracal, and Jennifer Lloyd for sending me materials I used to make the Marjorie Loman trial realistic.

I want to offer special thanks to my good friend Dr. Jeffrey Weiss, who crafted the technical aspects of

...od's direct and cross-examinations of ...t witnesses in the shaken baby case.

Next, continuing thanks to Jennifer Weltz, my superagent and first reader, super-duper agent emeritus Jean Naggar, and everyone else at the Jean V. Naggar Literary Agency who make it possible for me to earn a living doing something I love.

My books are a joint enterprise. If you enjoyed *The Darkest Place,* send a thank-you card to my fabulous editor, Keith Kahla, who corrects my mistakes and English. Thanks as always to the crew at St. Martin's: Hector DeJean, Martin Quinn, Alice Pfeifer, Sally Richardson, Andy Martin, Kelley Ragland, Sara and Chris Ensey, Ken Silver, David Rotstein, Matie Argiropoulos, and Theresa Plummer, the voice of Robin Lockwood.

Finally, a special thank-you to Melanie Nelson, my terrific wife, for putting up with me and making my life one big adventure.

Read on for an excerpt from *Murder at Black Oaks*– the next exciting novel by Phillip Margolin, available soon in hardcover from Minotaur Books!

Robin Lockwood and her fiancé, Jeff Hodges, were standing side by side in an elevator. Robin held up her hand and admired her engagement ring. She couldn't help smiling every time she looked at it. Jeff laughed. He was six foot two with shaggy, reddish-blond hair that Robin ran her hand through when they made love.

"You are so silly," Jeff said.

Robin leaned over and kissed Jeff just as the car stopped and the elevator door opened. The couple turned. A man was standing outside the car. He was holding a gun. Robin screamed, "No," and held out the hand with the ring. That's when the man fired, and Robin jerked up in bed, her heart pounding and her eyes wide open, drenched in sweat, and more tired than she'd been when she went to bed.

This was not the first night Robin had been dragged into a nightmare-filled sleep, but this evening her nightmare had been exceptionally vivid. That was probably because this was the two-year anniversary of the day a grief-stricken husband had accidentally gunned down Jeff at the sentencing hearing of another man who'd raped his wife.

Ever since Jeff had been killed, Robin had experienced vivid flashbacks that forced her to relive the unbearable grief she'd suffered, leaving her torn between a desire to have the pain stop and the fear that Jeff would vanish if it did.

Robin was five-foot-eight with a wiry build, clear blue eyes, a straight nose, high cheekbones, and short blond hair. She'd been a nationally ranked, mixed martial arts fighter in college, and she'd had a brief star turn as "Rockin' Robin" when she fought on TV in pay-per-view bouts, but she'd quit fighting professionally in her first year at Yale Law School after she had suffered a brutal knockout that resulted in a concussion and short-term memory loss.

After moving to Portland, Oregon, to join the firm that had become Barrister, Berman, and Lockwood, Robin stayed in shape by going to McGill's gym every workday morning to spar or pump iron before going to her office.

This morning, Robin didn't want to work out, but she knew she had to keep to her routine or risk falling into despair, so she got her breathing under control, fought back her tears, got into her workout gear, and ran to McGill's.

Portland's Pearl District had been a dusty, decaying area home to warehouses and populated by the homeless. Then the developers moved in and replaced the grimy, run-down warehouses with gleaming, high-end condos, trendy restaurants, and chic boutiques. McGill's gym took up the bottom floor of one of the few brick buildings that had escaped gentrification. It was dimly lit, smelled of sweat, and was home to professional boxers, MMA fighters, and serious bodybuilders.

Barry McGill had been a top middleweight many pounds ago and was one of Robin's favorite people.

"Your buddy's been here for half an hour, working out, while your sorry ass was still in bed," McGill said.

Robin was certain that Barry knew what day this was, and she was grateful that he was his usual abrasive self and hadn't mentioned Jeff or offered her condolences.

Robin walked over to the mat where Sally Martinez was waiting. Sally was a CPA, but she'd been a championship wrestler in college, who had just missed out on a spot on an Olympic team. After graduating, Sally had studied mixed martial arts. She was a few pounds heavier than Robin, but Robin had a few inches on her friend and they were pretty even in ability, although Robin had a slight edge.

"Sorry I'm late," Robin said.

"Not a problem. I don't have anything pressing at the office."

Sally knew that this was the anniversary of Jeff's death, and she came at Robin extra hard so her friend would be forced to focus. Robin was able to forget Jeff for an hour. Then the workout ended, and the two friends went into the locker room to change.

There were two shower stalls in the ladies' locker room. Robin stripped and went into one of them. As soon as she was alone, memories of Jeff cascaded over her. Robin turned on the shower, hoping that the din of the rushing water would drown out the sound of the sobs that made her chest heave and her heart hurt.

Robin heard Sally's shower stop, but she stayed in her stall. She didn't want her friend to see her like this. She didn't want pity, and she didn't want to burden anyone else with her pain.

"I'm headed out," Sally yelled.

"See you," Robin managed.

A few minutes after Sally left, Robin gathered herself and wiped away her tears. After she dried off, Robin put on the pants suit she kept in her locker and started the twenty-minute walk to her office.

The weather fit Robin's mood. It had rained last night, and there was still a threat of rain in the air.

Robin stopped for a latte and a scone at the coffee shop across from her office before taking the elevator to the offices of Barrister, Berman, and Lockwood.

Regina Barrister had been widely recognized as the best criminal lawyer in Oregon. Just before she retired after the onset of dementia, Regina had promoted Mark Berman and Robin to partnerships in the firm and left her practice in their hands.

Mark had graciously let Robin have Regina's corner office, which had spectacular views of the snow-capped peaks of Mount Hood and Mount St. Helens and the Willamette River, but today dark clouds hid the mountains from sight, and the rain was keeping most boats off the river.

Robin had hurt her shoulder when Sally executed a judo throw, and it was still aching when she closed the door to her office. She had just started to check her emails when her receptionist told her that she had a call.

"This is Robin Lockwood. How can I help you?"

"My name is Nelly Melville, and I'm calling for my father, Frank Melville. He has a legal matter he'd like to discuss with you."

"When would he like to come in?"

"That's the thing, Miss Lockwood. My father was in a terrible car accident several years ago. Katherine, his wife and my mother, was killed, and he was paralyzed from the waist down. He hasn't left Black Oaks since he got out of the hospital. It would be extremely difficult for my father to visit your office. Can you come here?"

"Where is Black Oaks?"

"It's on the top of Solitude Mountain, several hours from Portland. We're quite isolated, but the view is spectacular, and I think you'll find Black Oaks interesting. It's a re-creation of a famous manor house that's on the English moors. We've even got a curse attached to the place."

Robin was intrigued. "What does your father want to discuss with me?"

"I don't know. He refused to explain why he wants to see you. Whatever it is has really upset him. I know this is an imposition, but I assure you that you'll be well compensated for your time."

"Can you tell me a little more about your father?"

"You might have heard of him. I know you practice criminal law. He was one of the top prosecutors in the Multnomah County district attorney's office before he went into partnership with Lawrence Trent."

"I'm relatively new to Oregon, so the name doesn't ring a bell."

"Oh, if you haven't been here long, you probably wouldn't know Dad."

For a while, Robin had been able to dull the pain of losing Jeff by immersing herself in a few challenging cases, but her current caseload offered little mental stimulation. The mysterious summons had piqued her interest and going to Black Oaks would take her away from all the sights that were a constant reminder of Jeff.

"I can drive up Wednesday. Is that okay?"

"Thank you. My father will be very grateful. When you get close, phone the house." Nelly gave Robin the number of her cell and the Black Oaks landline. "Cell phone reception is spotty on the mountain, but there's a call box at the gate. Use it if your call doesn't go through. Oh, and pack a bag. You'll probably want to stay the night rather than drive back to Portland, but we have plenty of guest rooms and an excellent cook."

As soon as Robin disconnected, she used the intercom to summon Loretta Washington, one of her associates. Loretta was a five-foot-one, African American dynamo, with eyes the color of milk chocolate, who had recently started to style her hair in cornrows. Robin had nicknamed Loretta "The Flash," because she was always in motion.

Like Robin, Loretta was the first person in her family to graduate from college. She'd grown up in the Bronx, graduated from Queens College in New York, and traveled to Portland when she received a full ride from Lewis & Clark Law School. Loretta's hire had nothing to do with diversity. She had finished fifth in her class, had clerked on the Oregon Supreme Court, and was not only a brilliant appellate attorney but was showing promise as a trial lawyer. She was also fun to be around.

"What's up, boss?" Loretta asked as soon as she settled into a client chair across from Robin.

"I need you to tell me everything you can find out about a man named Frank Melville. He was a DA in Portland and a partner in Lawrence Trent's law firm. A few years ago, he was in a very bad car accident. His wife died, and he was seriously injured. He's wheelchair-bound, and he lives in Black Oaks on Solitude Mountain."

"Sounds spooky."

Robin smiled. "It does, doesn't it? An isolated mansion called Black Oaks on the top of a mountain named Solitude. That's right out of one of those old B movies that starred Bela Lugosi and Boris Karloff."

Loretta's brow furrowed. "Who?"

Jeff had been a movie buff, and he'd insisted that Robin watch *Dracula, Frankenstein, The Wolf Man,* and a raft of black-and-white horror classics.

"Look them up too. Consider it a part of your education."

"How soon do you need this? I'm knee-deep in the research in the *Kim* case."

"Pull yourself out of that quagmire and hop on this. I'm driving up Wednesday, so I need the info ASAP."

"I'll have it to you when you get in tomorrow."

By the time Robin went to bed, she was emotionally exhausted and had a deep, dream-free sleep. She felt a little better when she woke up, but her shoulder was still bothering her, so she decided to skip the gym.

Robin was excited about her mysterious mission to Black Oaks, and she was anxious to hear what Loretta had discovered. Her associate was waiting for Robin when Robin walked into her office the next morning carrying two lattes and two croissants.

"What do you know about werewolves?" Loretta asked after taking a bite of her croissant and a sip of the latte.

"Other than what I learned watching those old horror movies, not a lot."

"Then you better get up to speed if you're going to Black Oaks."

"And that is because . . . ?"

Loretta scooted up to the edge of her chair and leaned forward.

"Black Oaks is cursed. Everyone who has lived there has met a horrible end."

Robin smiled. "They get eaten by werewolves?"

"A few have, which should worry you."

Robin laughed. "You have my attention, Loretta. Please go on."

"In 1673, Angus McTavish built Black Oaks on a desolate part of the moors, several miles from Sexton, a small English village. McTavish had two sons. His wife and the youngest boy died from a plague that ravaged the area. Niles, the eldest son, began a career in the clergy, but was defrocked a year into his first posting. McTavish was the wealthiest man in the area, and the reasons for Niles's expulsion from the church were hushed up, but there were rumors that Niles had been experimenting with the occult.

"Soon after Niles moved back to Black Oaks, Angus went for a walk on the moors. When he didn't return, search parties were sent out." Loretta flashed a satanic grin. "They found his body. His throat had been torn out, and, according to a contemporaneous historical account, 'his face had a look of horror that haunted the dreams of all who looked upon him.'

"Niles McTavish took over Black Oaks as soon as his father was laid to rest, and the manor soon became the scene of—and I quote again—'debauched and drunken revels shunned by decent folk.' There were rumors that satanic rites were performed and orgies took place in the secret passageways and dungeon of the manor.

"Niles was denounced from the pulpit, but he had the local officials in his pocket, and nothing was done to curb his scandalous exploits. Given his reputation and the disgust with which he was viewed by the general public, you can imagine the dismay among the respectable elements of society when McTavish announced his betrothal to Alice Standish, the daughter of Ian Standish, Sexton's mayor. That 'Sweet Alice,' as she was called, would consent to marry Niles and that her father would not stand in the way of the match lent credence to the belief that witchcraft was involved. Of course, Ian might just have liked the idea of his daughter marrying a really rich guy."

"God, you're cynical," Robin said.

Loretta shrugged. "Law school trained me to look at both sides of an issue."

Robin laughed. "Continue."

"Okay. Well, two days of merrymaking preceded the wedding; read Spring Break Moors, with lots of drinking and lots of sex with devil worship thrown in for good measure.

"Niles had scheduled the wedding ceremony to take place at midnight. There's a legend that the Devil arrived at the stroke of twelve in a black coach drawn by seven coal-black horses and presented the groom with a carved wooden box engraved with a bloodred pentagram that contained a knife with a silver handle that looked like a claw that was half-human, half-wolf. The knife and the box actually existed. There were several witness accounts about that. But I couldn't find any cell phone shots of the Devil on Facebook or YouTube."

Robin laughed again. "I don't think you're taking this seriously."

Loretta smiled. "After midnight," she said, "the newlyweds retired to Niles's bedchamber. For days after, neither bride nor groom were seen. Meals were left outside the door, but, after the first day, they remained in the hall uneaten. A servant was always outside the door to receive orders. He reported hearing odd noises emanating from the room.

"When several days passed without Alice or Niles showing their faces, Alice's father demanded that Niles let him in. When he received no reply, he had the servants break down the door, and things got really weird."

"As if they weren't already," Robin interjected. Loretta's grin was positively ghoulish.

"Inside was a chamber of horrors. Alice was naked

and dead. Her throat had been ripped apart, and her body was drenched in blood. Niles was nowhere to be found.

"Alice's father went insane when he saw his daughter's mangled body. He tore the room apart and found a false wall that opened into a passage that led to the moors. A search party was formed. The members claimed that they had not been able to find Niles, but days later a hunter found his mangled body. He had been sliced to ribbons, and the knife with the werewolf handle was buried in his heart.

"Everyone suspected that Alice's father had done the deed, but every member of the search party swore that they had not found Niles. Ian lived in seclusion until he passed away a few years later."

"That's some story. What happened to Black Oaks?" Robin asked.

"Niles was the last of Angus McTavish's line, so there were no heirs. Given the bad vibes associated with Black Oaks, no one showed an interest in buying it or moving in, and the manor fell into disrepair. Over time, the village expanded and became a city, and the outer boundaries expanded until the city was less than a mile from Black Oaks. The Sexton Historical Society got a grant to restore it, and it became a museum and tourist attraction, which is how Katherine Melville, Nelly Melville's mother and Frank Melville's wife, discovered it.

"Katherine Melville inherited a vast family fortune that was made when logging was Oregon's main industry. She was obsessed with European history and became fascinated by the Black Oaks legend when she was studying at Oxford. When she got her inheritance, she decided to re-create Black Oaks in a remote area on Solitude Mountain. There are some modern additions, but most of the house on top of Solitude Mountain is a stone-by-stone re-creation of the original manor house in Sexton, England."

"What did you find out about Frank Melville?" Robin asked.

"There's a bit of a mystery here," Loretta said. "Melville was a DA in Multnomah County who specialized in prosecuting capital cases. After he left the DA's office, he joined Lawrence Trent's law firm. I talked with a friend at the firm. She told me that Melville was very successful, but a few years after going in with Trent he retired abruptly without giving a reason.

"Shortly after he retired, Frank and Katherine were in a terrible car accident. Katherine died, and Frank was paralyzed from the waist down. Melville has been living at Black Oaks since the accident, and he spends his time looking into the cases of convicted murderers who claim they're innocent. So far, his research has freed two men from prison.

"Frank and Katherine had one child, Nelly. She was

inspired by her mother's passion and got a degree in European history at Columbia before going to Oxford to pursue a graduate degree. After the crash, she gave up her studies and moved to Black Oaks to take care of her father."

"I wonder why Melville quit practicing," Robin said.

"You can ask him, if you're still going to Black Oaks after hearing about the devil worship and supernatural animals."

"I'm more determined than ever now."

"Then I would advise you to bring a crucifix, holy water, and a necklace of garlic to the spooky castle."

Robin shook her head. "And here I thought you were an ace researcher. The crucifix and that other stuff are for vampires. Werewolves can only be killed by silver bullets."

"My bad. So, you're going?"

"Only if there's no full moon tomorrow."